TAKEN 45 TIMES

45 MEN 10 WOMEN, YOU DO THE MATH

NICKI MENAGE   SAFFRON SANDS   AMBER GRAY

CHARLOTTE STORM   MARGOT DEVINE

PHILLIPA SAINT   ZOE MORRISON

STEPH BROTHERS   ELIZA DEGAULLE

CASSANDRA ZARA

Edited by

SCARLETT SKYES

SHAMELESS BOOK PRESS

Disclaimer

All characters and events are entirely fictional and any resemblances to persons living or dead and circumstances are purely coincidental. All sex acts depicted occur between characters 18 years or older.

CONTENTS

vetted than the eBook retailers are able to achieve. That said, the emails will be filled with erotica recommendations, so don't gather your friends and family around the computer when you read them if you don't want everybody to know what blows your hair back.

Professional: Shameless Book Deals is run by Scarlett Skyes, a #1 erotica author with an eye for quality erotica.

Quality: All authors/publishers are expected to hold to a high standard for their work and the deals they are offering to our subscribers. Check the Newsletter Submission Guidelines and report any authors that you believe have breached these guidelines. We recognize that not all complaints will be valid, but authors/publishers who are repeat offenders will be blacklisted to maintain the quality of our service.

Free Stories: Every subscriber gets access to a selection of FREE, and in some cases exclusive, erotica. Downloadable directly from our website.

WELCOME TO THE HOUSE OF FUN
BY NICKY MENAGE

When I lose my friend Marie at the local theme-park I go in search of her in the seemingly abandoned fun-house. The insides tell a different story though and I soon find myself amidst a sinful game, with glory-holes and hot guys abound. Read as I have my first taste of what a gang session is like, taking on four hunks—the cop, the biker, the cowboy and the construction-worker—all to myself!

I emerged from the restroom, walking back into the hustle and bustle of the noisy, busy theme-park. Marie had told me she'd wait outside, but for now I couldn't see her.

I thought perhaps we'd somehow passed each other inside so I waited a while longer, watching as families and friends laughed their way through the park.

After a few minutes I became more suspicious. I checked my phone and gave Marie a call but there was no answer.

I started to smile, thinking that perhaps she was waiting

and watching me the entire time, but as I turned my head and looked to benches and bushes there was still no sign of her.

"Huh," I hummed, and I began to stroll off slowly in the direction I thought she might have taken.

The main body of the park lay behind me and from here the pathways tapered off somewhat to some of the less popular rides.

"Marie," I called now that the noise of the park was behind me, but still no sound returned.

The trees grew closer to the pathway as I continued to stroll and this part of the park seemed all but desolate. The only sign of life lay in the form of an old fun-house, with human-sized hamster wheels and roller-pin sidewalks along its front porch.

"Hello?" I called again, steadily approaching the seemingly abandoned house.

A sign above the door read 'Entrance.' I found myself drawn to it, thinking that perhaps so too had Marie.

"Marie?" I called again. "Are you in there?"

I waited on the metal steps that led up to the doorway, listening out for any faint reply. None came.

"Marie?" I spoke again.

I looked back to the path that had led me here to see it still deserted. The odd passer-by could be seen beyond, but no-one ventured down here. I could see why.

"If you're in there ..." I warned, and I stepped in through the long flaps of plastic that covered the doorframe.

Inside the room was softly lit with blue and purple lights. There was a strange smell in the air—but not an unpleasant one—and a low hum seemed to ring out all over.

"Welcome to the House of Fun!" a voice chimed over an address system. "What is it you desire today?"

I furrowed my brow in confusion. "*What is it I desire?* Four hot guys, how do you like that? Then afterwards maybe I can find my friend. Marie?!"

I walked through the first room and to the doorway on the opposite side. I pushed my way through it into another room that seemed even larger.

The light in here flashed wildly in a strobe effect. It would illuminate brightly and then fall dark, leaving me in a state of bewilderment. I half-thought of turning back.

Regardless I pushed on. I'm not sure what compelled me, but I couldn't shake the feeling that Marie had been here. I couldn't explain it.

I put a foot out in front of me and it struck something invisible. My hand reached out and I touched a clear sheet of plastic that seemed to divide the room.

"Great," I laughed.

I walked like Frankenstein's monster keeping both hands out in front of me and feeling my way slowly ahead as the lights in the room turned on and off.

Something flashed in the corner of my eye and I looked up to see what had alerted me. The light blinked on. Nothing. Off and then on. Nothing. Off and then on. *Someone.*

"Hello!" I cried.

In the intermittent flash the figure had gone, but the lingering image was one of a bare-chested man, standing a few feet away from me and on the other side of two corridors of plastic sheeting.

I made my way steadily towards the figure. Looking back now I should have been terrified, but my pervading emotion was of intrigue and confusion. If there was a half-naked buff guy in here then Marie could wait! I hadn't gotten any in a while.

"Hey!" I called out again, coming to the spot where the guy had appeared.

I could hear the beat of some brisk music beyond and as I

stepped through into the adjacent room the sound became louder. *Someone* was here.

The room I stood in now was filled with mirrors of different shapes and bends. It distorted my reflection wildly. In one mirror I was a tall, leggy blonde with denim-clad pins that stretched all the way up to my tight ass.

In another mirror I was a short, curvy blonde whose breasts pushed out as far on one side of my profile as my ass did on the other.

"Looking good," came a smooth, male voice and in the corner of the mirror I caught yet another reflection.

I turned quickly and this time the figure stayed. It was a guy of about thirty-something wearing an open leather jacket and matching leather pants.

"Lost your motorbike?" I joked.

He laughed and pushed his back off of the wall to stand upright. His hands stayed in his pockets and for a moment it looked like he was posing as the centerfold in a woman's dirty magazine.

"Have you seen my friend?" I asked.

The guy didn't answer. Instead he left me an alluring look and turned for the door of the room.

"Hey!" I cried after, but he didn't stop.

I moved quickly after him, pushing through the flaps of plastic to be met with another empty room.

"You gotta be fucking kidding me?" I laughed.

This room was like the first: lit lowly and with these fabric-lined walls and floors—as though the whole thing was soundproofed.

I was so perplexed at the sudden disappearance of my buff biker that I didn't even notice the glory-holes that adorned the walls around the outside of the room.

"What is going on in here?" I asked, and the music seemed to get dialed up a notch.

From the corner of my eye I spotted something else and my head turned to it in a flash, fearful that it might soon disappear and leave me with a ton of questions once more. So unexpected was the sight that greeted me that it took a while for it to register.

"Is that …" I began, cocking my head.

"A cock," a voice came. I turned to it to see the biker, propped with his shoulders against the corner of the room. "A nice, hard cock. Just for you."

"For me?!" I said, hand on chest.

He nodded simply and I looked back to the protruding length. It was big—big enough to lurch into the room and make its presence more than known. Not only that but it looked beautiful, as though someone had sculpted it with a mind to creating the perfect penis.

"All yours if you want it," the biker said.

The thoughts of Marie couldn't have left my mind faster. I was a good friend to her—don't get me wrong—but who could really be in any kind of danger in the middle of a busy theme-park?

My eyes focused on the appendage and the beat of the music grew louder in my ear, as though it was building towards my decision.

"Whose is it?" I asked, looking back to the biker.

I'd half expected him to have vanished, but instead he'd moved closer behind me. He stood there, his face smooth and close shaven, matching his waxed, muscled chest that showed out beneath his silver-zippered leatherjacket.

"It's my friend's," he said. "And there's more where that came from."

He nodded back to the wall and I turned again, watching as two more stiff, primed cocks emerged. One was like the first, but the second was black and inviting.

"Whichever one you so choose …" the biker said, as though he was some kind of adult mystic.

"I can't believe this!"

I laughed, but only briefly. The sight of three engorged cocks was just too much to take in. I felt my pussy turn hot beneath my jeans and my heart started to race with excitement.

"Are you sure I can just … suck one?"

"Sure as hell," the biker responded. "They won't mind. Why do you think they're there?"

I raised an eyebrow. "Huh."

I looked along the chorus-line of cocks and walked between each as the biker watched me choose. I half-though about doing a game of eenie-meenie but in the back of my mind I knew what the answer was. I wanted the cock that was least like the others. I'd never been with a black guy before.

"This one," I said, standing before it. It bobbed as though its owner knew my selection.

"Good choice," the biker said, moving again towards me. He stood on my shoulder, like a giant fairy, whispering his sinful suggestions in my ear.

"On your knees then," he said, brushing back my hair and putting his mouth closer to my lobe. "On your knees and suck that hard, black cock."

I fell forwards and lunged for it like an animal. From behind the wall I heard a hiss of breath as I threw my lips over it, driving as much of it as I could into me.

"Good," the biker encouraged.

I felt the tip of him arrive at my throat but I didn't care. I managed to stifle the gag and keep him in the tight clasp of my gullet, long enough for me to hear him rejoice again on the other side of the divide.

"That's so fucking good," the biker declared, and he said the words so headily that I had to turn to look back at him.

I noticed that he'd unzipped his pants and through his fly sat another perfect-looking, hard cock. He took it in his hands and started to beat it slowly.

"Don't mind me," he said.

"How can I not?!"

"You focus on keeping them hard," he said, nodding to the line of dicks. "I can take care of myself. For now…"

He let the statement linger with a smirk and I grinned in response. I turned back to the big black cock that throbbed in my grasp and sent it back into my mouth, jerking on the lower shaft that I couldn't claim with my lips.

"Fuck," came a grunt from beyond the wall.

I looked down along the line to see the other two lonely cocks, seemingly demanding of attention as they stood proudly. How could I refuse?

I shuffled on my knees along the floor and arrived at the middle cock. At first I fondled the balls with my finger tips and I watched with relish as the cock above tensed up and shook firmly.

"You now," I hushed, and I moved my mouth towards it to kiss lovingly on the thick barrel. I couldn't fucking believe it, but in the moment every action of mine seemed somehow *right*.

It seemed as though there were no inhibitions or judgment in that Fun-House and it truly felt like my heart's desires were within my grasp. Quite literally!

I looked down along the barrel of flesh and drove my lips over it, feeling like the naughtiest kind of slut in the world.

The black cock to my right and the white one to my left lay in wait. I reached out and grabbed both, rocking my head over the cock in the middle and jerking the two on either side of it in unison.

My stomach swelled with desire and I felt the adrenaline pump through my veins. It felt as though I was fulfilling a wish that I didn't truly know I held. Three men at once was something that none of my friends had ever done, and when the fourth cock arrived on my shoulder I knew just what to do.

"You too, huh?" I asked, looking back up at the biker. He stared down expectantly and I didn't want to disappoint.

I took that majestic cock of his in my midst and jerked it hard, driving my mouth over the tip and keeping it over him as my hand pumped along his stiffness.

My tongue swirled around the tip of him and I let out a pleasured cry. I reached out for the cock behind me but my hand found nothing. I fumbled against the fabric wall a while longer before finally turning to see it empty and the holes abandoned.

"They're gone?" I asked. "Just like that?"

"Not quite," the biker said.

Suddenly a figure entered the room in a cowboy hat and a set of chaps, only without the pants that were supposed to be underneath. Instead his hard cock bounced between his legs, and the film of saliva around it told me that it had very recently been in my mouth.

"My, my," I swooned, knelt on the floor all vulnerable-like.

Behind the cowboy there followed a tall black guy with an unmistakable cock shaking on his hips. He wore a set of aviators and a police-helmet, with polished boots and a belt with a Billy-club attached.

"You guys remind me of someone…" I said, narrowing my eyes to think where I'd seen this trio before.

Before I could place them a fourth guy arrived in a bright neon safety-vest, heavy boots and a hard-hat.

"The biker, the cop, the construction-worker and the

cowboy," I said, looking up at the four of them as they surrounded me. "It's my lucky day."

"Ours too," said the cop, holding his cock and steering it towards me.

"Get back inside me," I said dreamily, and I put my hands on my thighs and opened my mouth to receive him.

The three other gents jerked steadily as I tackled the cop, driving my lips down along that thick barrel and fondling his balls as I toyed with him.

The guys would switch positions often, and I'd give each of them a turn in my mouth. Eventually I became braver and started to jerk two of the other cocks, leaving the fourth guy to fend for himself before his turn was due.

I was like a champion plate-spinner, only instead of the fear of breaking crockery I had the imminent threat of one of the guys in my care softening.

Truthfully it wasn't a worry. The testosterone and excitement in the room saw to that. Each cock was as hard as the other and stayed that way. Whenever I found them in my mouth it felt as though I was sucking on something more akin to rock.

"I'm afraid I'm gonna have to write you up," the cop said now, patting his club into his open palm.

"For what, officer?" I asked, playing his game.

"For wearing entirely too many clothes," he smirked.

"I think we can fix that," the cowboy said.

"In no time," the construction worker added.

The biker helped me to my feet and I stood in the center of all of them. I'd never felt so wanted. Their hands started to move over me and it was hard to discern which of them was squeezing at my tits or ass. It was like sensory overload.

"You're spoiling me," I hushed, turning in the circle.

"We haven't started yet, miss," the cop said.

A pair of hands arrived at the bottom of my t-shirt and

soon the garment was being pulled upwards. I raised my hands and felt my top slip up over my breasts. As soon as it did I felt a pair of hands grip my tits, pushing the bra against them and bunching my assets together.

My shirt was tossed aside and I stared with sparkling eyes at the cowboy who looked longingly at my big breasts. His heavy hands felt good on me.

"Don't be shy, boys," I breezed.

My confidence was immeasurable. Being wanted by one guy made me feel pretty good, but being in a room full of guys who wanted me was like nothing else. And I can tell you I wanted them too. I wanted each of them in turn or perhaps together. The sheer possibilities drove me wild with excitement.

Their hands moved over me in sliding waves, touching in places that I hadn't been touched in a long time. I felt a hand slip down the back of my jeans and take a fistful of my ass, then another popped open the button of my jeans and slid down the zipper.

I groaned as the biker started to kiss at my neck, biting little love-bites on my skin that juxtaposed the roughness of the other men.

My jeans were pulled down over my ass as I let them all have their way with me—and have their way with me they did.

Before I knew it I was being helped out of my jeans and sneakers, but the buff construction-worker that knelt down to aid me didn't stand back up. Instead he rubbed at my thighs and stared ahead at the thin fabric of my lacey panties. Thankfully I'd worn a pair I was proud of!

"Look at that," he hushed.

"Go for it," the biker encouraged, and I could hear his caramel voice against my ear. It sent a shiver down my spine.

"Please," I hushed, staring down at the man on his knees.

I reached out and gripped at two of the cocks around me, tugging along them as best I could as the face of the bright-vested worker arrived between my legs.

First of all I felt his breath on me—warm and inviting—then I felt the touch of his lips as he started to kiss my panties.

"Yes," I gushed, putting my hand on the smooth hard-hat and pulling him closer.

He responded with a flailing tongue that rushed across my pussy and I gripped tighter at the cocks of the cowboy and the cop in my midst.

"Eat that pussy," the cop cheered, looking down to his friend who smiled with his eyes. His mouth was far too busy.

I breathed deep and heavy, falling back against the biker who held me and gripped my tits in the process.

My hands rifled along the cocks in front of me and I felt the finger of the construction-worker curl under the crotch of my panties.

He moved them aside and now his flesh touched mine for real. I groaned loud enough for my cries to bounce off the walls. My pussy swelled with excitement and my clit stiffened, sought-out quickly by the ravenous tongue at my folds.

"Fuck me," I urged.

"Oh, we'll get to that," the cowboy said.

The biker's toned chest pressed against my back and he pulled at the cups of my bra. They slid down to reveal my big tits and pink nipples that proved just too inviting for the cowboy and the cop.

As though they were one, the two men dropped their heads and clamped their mouths over my nipples. I could feel the stubble of the cowboy graze my soft, milky skin and the tongues of each were as dexterous as the other.

They turned my nipples stiff in seconds and continued to

swirl around them, sending shivers of excitement rattling through me.

My thighs trembled as the mouth of the guy at my feet worked busily. He'd slide his tongue up and down my folds and then probe with a finger, coaxing out the hot cum that lay in wait inside me.

"Yes!" I shuddered, my jaw trembling.

The biker unfastened the clasp of my bra and took it off my arms. His friends vacated my chest briefly to see the garment removed, then instantly resumed their fill on my big tits.

"Good girl," the biker said from behind, kissing at my back while his stiff cock pressed against my ass.

The construction-worker took the waist of my panties now and pulled them down, slipping them over the soft, smooth skin of my legs until they were at the floor.

I stepped out of them and felt the biker pull away from me. He angled his meaty cock up along the crease of my ass and then returned to hug me close, sandwiching his length against my back.

I tugged on the cowboy and the cop as they feasted on my tits, relishing the stiffness that each of them displayed.

"Oh, fuck!" I groaned, feeling my pussy quiver.

I looked down at the face of the construction-worker as he pleased me. His eyes were closed and he was focusing hard, swirling himself along my folds. I had no doubt that he could feel the contractions of my pussy against his mouth and it seemed only to drive me on further.

"I'm gonna come," I announced, and all of the men around me became more animated.

"Come," the biker hushed, grinding his dick along the cleavage of my ass.

He dropped to his knees behind me. I didn't give it any thought to begin with—so enamored was I by his friend at my pussy—but when I felt a hand split my ass and then a tongue collide with my tiny knot ... well it just drove me fucking wild!

I cried out passionately, pushing back against the biker's face while his friend opposite moved closer to my retreating pussy.

"Fuck!" I grunted, and the climax started to flow out of me.

The cowboy held me steady as my legs turned weak, and the tongues of the biker and the construction-worker probed fiercely.

My asshole was winking as the contractions flowed out of me. Each man ate ravenously and it was tough to focus. My head fell light as I sucked in deep breaths and the room started to fog and cloud with colors.

"Yes!" I squeaked.

My whole body tensed and flexed before relaxing so heavily that I almost fell off my feet. The cop and cowboy held me steady, still delighting my nipples as their friends struck at my pussy and ass.

The cream of my sex flowed freely and the construction-worker lapped it up hungrily. I was so soaked from the both of them but I didn't want it to stop there.

"Now it's your turn," I breathed, giddy and briefly exhausted.

"Where do you want us?" the cop asked.

I took a moment to think. I was like a child in a sweet shop asking what she wanted to eat first. Everything seemed so good that it was tough to decide.

"I think it's only fair that the biker goes in my ass," I said, surprising myself.

The cop raised his eyebrows. "Lucky guy."

"He's done such a sterling job," I giggled, looking back down behind me at him.

He kissed my ass adoringly.

"And you," I said, holding the face of the cop. "I want that thick thing in my pussy."

The construction-worker stood up, wiping at his face. I pulled on his safety-jacket and when he was close I gave him a big, wet kiss. I could taste my sweetness on his lips.

"Thank you," I hushed. "Those lips of yours are quite the asset."

"I do what I can," he said modestly, and the cowboy gave him a playful slap on the back.

"Where do you want us?" the cowboy asked, smiling eagerly.

"You two …" I said, putting a finger to my lips to think. "I think I want you both at my face. I want to suck it out of you and take it all over me."

Their eyes widened. "Right you are," the construction-worker said.

The music pounded as the biker lay back on the floor, angling his cock upwards and waiting.

"Your chariot awaits," the cop said, presenting his supine friend to me.

"Never had a guy in my ass before," I smiled.

"Never had four guys either, I imagine," the cowboy joked.

"Let's see what happens," I giggled.

I squatted down towards the target slowly and the biker held himself upright. I put my hands on the thighs of his leather pants and then felt his hard, swollen tip as it stroked over my virginal knot.

I looked about the men that stood around me and each of them watched close, paying careful attention to the union of our sinful flesh.

"Look at her go," the cowboy swooned.

I laughed bashfully and then let out an "oooh" as I felt my muscle open to let him inside.

"Yes," the cop said, staring at my waiting pussy above. "Get inside her."

I dropped slowly and claimed the biker's inches. More and more of him drove into me until I could feel him in the pit of my stomach. As I engulfed him slowly I felt a giddy sense of power and relief. I'd never had anyone in there before.

"Good girl," the biker said, holding my ass off him. Steadily he pushed upwards and gave me the last of himself then I dropped back down with him and sat on his waist.

I blew a jet of air up my face. "Now who's next?"

The cop strode forward, jerking his cock slowly and pinching to the tip. "That'd be me, ma'am."

"Get in me," I said with a smirk.

I watched as the guy dropped to the floor. I could see my reflection in his aviators. I shivered with excitement and my eyes drifted down to his huge cock that came ever closer to my pussy as he approached.

"Ever had two guys inside you?" he asked.

"Never," I hushed, and the huge black cock washed up and down my folds.

"Here's to your first time," he said, and he pushed forwards.

I let out a groan as I felt the pressure of his girth against me. My pussy spread over him and he plunged deep, feeling tighter than any guy I'd ever had before in my life.

"So fucking tight," he hissed, "and so fucking wet."

He pushed onwards and I watched as his cock disappeared from view. My insides felt wholesomely full, like nothing I'd ever experienced. It was as though there'd been a life-long hole inside me that was only becoming apparent now that it was filled.

"Two men at once," the cowboy said. "How about three?"

I giggled briefly before the last inch of the cop took my breath away. The cowboy joined me along with the construction-worker and soon two more cocks were within my grasp.

"First come, first served," I said, grabbing the cowboy's cock and driving him into my mouth.

I started to bounce steadily and the cop took charge, sinking his big dick through my tight, vice-like pussy over and over.

Beneath me the biker stayed stiff, circled by my clamping muscle. I'd move over him when the strong thrusts of the bull-like cop hit me, and I'd feel the hard cock stir in my ass.

"You're a real naughty slut, huh?" the cop said.

"Just like the last one," the construction-worker said.

"The last one?" I asked.

"She's fine," the biker said. "Don't worry."

If I was honest I'd forgotten about Marie completely, but there was solace in knowing that she was fine. I could really enjoy myself now.

"I want you to fill me," I dared.

"You do, huh?" the biker said.

"All of you," I said. "I want all of your cum."

"You're gonna get it," the construction-worker said, beating his cock close to my face.

I gave him a quick suck and then looked up to his stubbled, handsome face. "You wanna come inside me too, stud?"

He bit at his lip and nodded.

"After," I said. "Let's get this fine cop's cum first."

The black policeman smiled his pearly whites at me and continued to thrust through my core. I could feel the pistons of each of my conquerors inside me, vacating and filling me in a joyous tag-team that I'd never forget.

"Just tell me when you want it," the cop said. "I'm ready when you are."

"I want your cum now," I said, staring at my reflection in his sunshades. "I want to feel it fill me."

A brief pang of worry hit inside me, but it was quickly doused by the excitement of it all. I couldn't start thinking about pregnancy now! All that mattered was the immediate sensations and then afterwards maybe I could consider the danger of it all.

"You want this big load?" he asked, watching as my pussy claimed his black thickness again and again.

"I do! Treat me like your slut and fill me."

"Fuck yeah!" he rejoiced, and then his lip curled and his head fell back.

I looked to my pussy and watched his cock throb, then I felt the rich heat fill me. The cop looked down at the source of his joy and fed himself through me slowly. Now his thrusts were lubricated by his slippery seed and felt even more joyous. He rubbed slowly against his biker friend inside me.

The cop pulled out with a grunt and stared at my gaping pussy. Inside the cum webbed over my folds and the construction-worker quickly jumped into the now vacant spot between my legs.

He jerked himself and looked at the creamy deposit of his friend. The cop was now moving to my mouth for some much-needed after-care.

I bounced faster on the biker's cock as I cleansed the policeman's length of his cum. My mouth raced down and my tongue swirled around his girth, lapping him up greedily until there was nothing left to claim.

"You gonna fill me too, big boy?" I asked, looking down underneath me.

The biker's eyes were closed as he focused on my tight

knot running up and down his length. It was as though I was jerking him with only the pinch of my asshole, and he looked to be absolutely enraptured by it.

"Fill my ass with your cum," I pleaded.

"Yes, ma'am," the biker grunted, and then his eyes opened wide and he breathed quick and deep.

"Yes!" I cried, bouncing faster and feeling him begin to fill me.

The heat was now in my pussy and my ass, with both holes being flooded with the seed of my band of strangers.

"You," I called, nodding to the brightly dressed worker. "In my pussy!"

My confidence bloomed as the eager construction-worker moved forward, jerking his weighty cock and then angling it towards my cum-soaked core.

He slipped through easily and quickly got up to speed, hammering into me with a wet clapping noise.

My asshole massaged out the last few drops of the biker and then I sat on him to drive his seed as deep as I could.

Cocks hit my face but now my eyes were closed. I wailed out my joy and kissed at whatever was presented before me. I could only tell the difference between each guy because the cop's cock still held the bitter, salty sweetness of his release across it.

"Fuuuuck!" the worker cried, and then I felt a third cock start to cum within me.

It throbbed wildly and my head turned floaty once-more. The cum of my two conquerors mingled inside me, doubling the danger of everything.

"I'm such a slut!" I cried, laughing.

"You love it," the cowboy laughed, jerking himself close to me. "Just tell me when you're ready."

He beat himself quickly close to my face. I didn't want him to hold off any longer.

"Now," I said. "Come all over my—"

Before I'd finished the sentence I heard a groan and then felt the lashing of heat crash across my face.

"Yes!" I groaned.

"What a cum-slut," someone said.

My eyes closed tight and I moaned gleefully, feeling a strange euphoria as the last cumshot blasted all hot over my face while the penultimate one continued in my pussy.

His seed fell into my mouth and I spat it out so that it rolled off down my chin and onto my big tits.

"Good job," the cop said, impressed at his friend's load.

The cowboy pumped the lashings from himself until my face was coated in a latticework of spunk. I breathed heavily and took the last few drops, then I opened my eyes cautiously and felt the cum spread over my lashes.

The cowboy thumbed his seed aside and I blinked carefully, smirking up at the two men who looked down on me now.

"Nice shot," the construction-worker said.

I eased up steadily and was reminded of the thickness in my ass that stayed hard. Gradually he slipped from me and I felt the contours of his cock run free.

My asshole winked shut and trapped the seed inside, but my pussy was less water tight. Some of the men's love dribbled from me and down my leg, but much, much more of them lay inside. I could tell from their throbs that the load was bounteous and I felt the briefest of panics at just how I would explain a pregnancy to someone.

'Whose is it?' I imagined someone asking.

'Well it could either be a cop's or a construction-worker's ...'

That'd go down well!

"We'll let you be on your way now, ma'am," one of the quartet said.

The cop helped me to my feet and each man in turn gave

me a kiss, finishing with the biker. They were careful not to touch the salty release of their friend that slid down slowly off my still-gasping face.

"You can clean up in the next room," the biker said.

I looked to the door and one of the men pushed me onwards, as though there was another woman waiting for the same treatment after me.

"You take care now," the cowboy said, tipping his hat.

I took up my clothes and moved through to a bright room with a sink and mirror. In the corner stood Marie, dressing slowly.

"Chelsea!" she cried, looking immediately to my cum-covered face.

"I—I—"

"Wild, wasn't it?" Marie said. "The Native-American guy really knows how to drill an ass."

I saw that Marie was still half-undressed, and the flushed red hue on her cheeks told me only one thing.

"You were in there before me?" I asked, aghast.

"Sure was," she said. "I didn't let them cum on my face though."

I pursed my lip and smiled, beginning to laugh. "That was fucking wild."

"You're telling me?!" Marie said.

"Best ride in the park, without doubt!"

Marie ran her eyes over my naked body and then slid her tongue over her teeth. "Should we go around again? Together?"

My eyes sparkled. "Might as well get our money's worth…"

THE END

GET ACCESS TO OVER 20 MORE FREE EROTICA DOWNLOADS AT SHAMELESS BOOK DEALS

Shameless Book Deals is a website that shamelessly brings you the very best erotica at the best prices from the best authors to your inbox every day. Sign up to our newsletter to get access to the daily deals and the Shameless Free Story Archive!

When Lana married Burt she had no idea how quickly her bright future could turn dark. Upon discovering her husband owed a rather ruthless character, she innocently agreed to help him get out of trouble.
But what Lana had quickly agreed to would change their marriage forever. She would have to sacrifice her dignity, her naivete, and of course her body in order to save her husband...but would she be able to return to the mediocre after tasting the erotic venture of five men at once?

*A*s I followed Burt into the dimly lit room, I felt the urge to turn and run away. But, I had agreed to partake in this debauchery, so I held his hand a little tighter as I let him lead me toward the bed in the center of the room.

At only twenty-three, a young bride of a powerful real estate mogul's son, I quickly discovered that I was more than a little naive about how the world worked. We had only been married for eight months and here I was, facing one of the darkest moments a relationship could have. I found myself sacrificing my body for my husband's mistakes.

I honestly loved Burt, so when he told me how much trouble he was in, I immediately told him I would do anything to help him....but that was before I had known how indebted he was to the most ruthless, so-called businessman I had ever heard of.

So here I was, willingly being led into a room with a bed where Burt would leave me with a group of five men that I did not know. I was to allow them to take me, use my body as they wanted...a gang bang that would pay off my husband's debts and release him from a contract with a major thug.

Burt motioned for me to sit on the bed. I sat on the silky red sheets, my hand trembling as I caressed the cool material in an attempt to soothe my anxiety.

I could see the straps at the corners of the bed. My heart raced, my mouth went dry as my anxiousness began to consume me. I was about to ask Burt to take me away when I heard a door open. I turned, staring into the darkness as the sound of footsteps echoed in the room. Straining my eyes, I tried to get a look at who was approaching.

I could hear the men speaking but not what they were saying as multiple shadowy figures stopped just before coming into my view.

I turned to look at Burt, pleading with my eyes for him to comfort me. "It's okay," he said with a smile. He stroked my hair and swept a stray tendril from my face.

I glanced over my shoulder at the door, then back to Burt as the men stepped to the foot of the bed.

I knew I was trembling as I looked up at the men, their eyes were full of lust, each of them grinning a sinister curl to their lips as they looked me up and down.

"She is just as pretty as you said," a man said as he lit a cigarette. The other four men nodded in agreement.

The man with the cigarette moved toward me. He grinned and licked his lips as he leaned forward. He sniffed loudly, inhaling my scent before stepping back. He continued to smile as he rearranged his cock in his pants. "Yeah, she will do just fine," he said to no one in particular.

The other four men began removing their clothes as I sat silent not knowing what to do.

"Now, Jacob, remember our deal," Burt said with a quiver in his voice, as he stepped between me and the man with the cigarette.

"No permanent marks. I got it." He gently pushed Burt to the side. "We will return her just as you brought her." He glanced over at the other men and chuckled. "Maybe a little looser." The men laughed as they tossed the rest of their clothing to the floor. "Are you staying for the show or picking her up when we are done?" Jacob said as he removed his jacket and tossed it aside.

"Don't leave me," I said without thinking and reached for my husband.

"I'll be back. I promise," Burt said then turned on his heels walking quickly out of the room.

I stared at where my husband had disappeared. He was gone. He had actually abandoned me, leaving me to the wolves. I could hear the men's breathing changing. They were excited, salivating at the chance to have their way with me.

"Relax and try to have a good time," Jacob said in a breathy voice.

I looked at him. Jacob was now naked along with the other four men. He was stroking himself as he moved closer to me. I scurried back onto the bed putting distance between me and Jacob.

Jacob laughed. "We can do this the easy way and you will

get as much pleasure from this as we will, or the hard way, and we will get even more pleasure out from you."

The men all laughed as I tried not to show my fear. My inner voice tried to soothe me. I heard my mind telling me to relax. One of my biggest sexual fantasies was to be the object of a gang bang, and here I was about to be fucked by five total strangers.

I licked my lips. "Can I at least have a drink before the festivities begin?" I said trying my best to not sound as terrified as I felt.

Jacob nodded. "Of course." He snapped his fingers and one of the guys, a muscular, dark haired man, trotted out of the room.

I stared as the other four stroked their cocks, my pussy twitching in anticipation even though my mind was still in full blown panic.

The door opened and my heart skipped a beat. Part of me actually held out hope it was Burt coming back to get me, but it wasn't. It was the man returning with my drink.

"Jack on the rocks." he said as he handed me a glass filled to the rim. "Figured a strong one was in order." He winked.

"No one else is having one?" I said with a tremble in my voice.

"Maybe after," Jacob said as he watched my shaky hand lift the glass to my lips.

It was indeed strong. I could feel the burn of the alcohol before I took my first sip. I shuddered as I swallowed. "Thanks." I raised my glass toward the man with the dark hair that had served my drink. I took a big gulp, and then another before handing my glass to Jacob.

"Feeling a little more at ease?" he asked as he gripped my arm and pulled me to the edge of the bed.

I softly said, "Yes," because I knew it was expected of me, but in reality I was still terrified.

~

FIVE MEN STOOD AROUND ME, cocks in hand, each rock-hard erection eager to be shoved inside me.

I swallowed hard as Jacob pulled me to my feet. I stood before him, my legs weak with a wild mixture of anticipation and apprehension. My breathing became shallow as he placed his hands on my shoulders. With a quick jerk, Jacob ripped my shirt open to reveal my breasts. I stood as tall as I could, my attempt at being defiant before the men began having their way with me. Staring up at Jacob, I fought the urge to cry though I knew the trembling of my bottom lip let him know how frightened I felt deep inside.

"Shhh...." Jacob whispered as his hands caressed the mounds of flesh spilling over my bra. "Try to enjoy it, baby." He placed his hand behind my neck, gripped a wad of my hair, and pulled my mouth to his.

At first I struggled, my hands in fists as I pressed them against his bare chest. But Jacob didn't let up. He held me firmly to him, his cock pressed up against me, his lips on mine as he forced his tongue inside my mouth.

I groaned and squirmed but that only made Jacob hold me tighter. His kiss became more forceful, his five o'clock shadow burning my delicate skin, but something about the forcefulness of his kiss fanned a tiny flame inside me. No man had ever kissed me with so much desire. For a moment I began to relax, to melt in his arms, and that is when Jacob pushed me to the mattress.

"Isaac," Jacob said and the curly-haired man that had brought me my drink was now standing over me. "Remove our guest's clothing." A smirk curled his lips as he watched Isaac get on the bed and pull my shirt the rest of the way off.

I didn't know how to react, so I turned my head to the

side, eyes closed as I felt my clothing being torn from my body.

I could feel the cool air on my skin as I now lay there, naked, even more vulnerable to their advances.

"Should I strap her down?" I heard Isaac say.

I looked at Jacob, my eyes wide with fear. "Please don't tie me up," I said. I'd rather be cooperative than incapacitated.

"No." Jacob put his hand up and motioned for the other guys to approach the bed. "We can have more fun with Lana if she has mobility."

Somehow that relieved me, at least until I felt hands all over my body, pulling me in so many directions I thought I might break.

My legs were spread wide, a man holding each leg, Isaac behind me, Jacob between my legs. Without a word his fingers were on my mound parting my labia, and then thrusting his fingers in and out of my pussy.

He pulled his fingers from inside me, licked the juices from them then dipped his fingers back deep inside me. "It seems to me you like this more than you are letting on, Lana." I chewed at my bottom lip refusing to respond to his comment. "Don't be shy. Burt left you here with us." He shook his head. "I can't believe he abandoned his beautiful young wife to the wolves."

I heard a tongue clicking and the man holding my left leg pulled at my nipple. "Don't worry. We won't tell him you like being fucked." He pinched my nipple then slapped my breast causing me to let out a squeal.

"Mmmm..." Jacob moved forward and slapped my pussy with his cock.

I stared up at him. Things were about to get real now. I closed my eyes, scrunching my face as I prepared to be filled with the first of five stranger's cocks.

"Oh, no, no," Jacob said. "Open those eyes and watch me

sink my cock inside your sweet pussy." He growled and Isaac yanked my hair, turning me to face Jacob.

"Do as you are told," Isaac said and yanked my hair once more.

I opened my eyes, stared at Jacob and watched as he forcefully thrust his cock inside me. I let out a soft whimper. It hurt having him shove his cock in deep with no warning, but strangely, it also felt good.

Mouths were now on my nipples, suckling, biting, and viciously pulling as Jacob continued to pump my pussy harder and harder. I tried not to struggle. My first instinct was to get him to come fast and get on with the next guy so I could be done with this entire gang bang ordeal. And then I remembered. I had stopped taking my birth control pills. Fear consumed me. I had wanted to become pregnant, but Burt was still reluctant. I had been 'forgetting' to take my pills in hopes of 'accidentally' becoming pregnant. And now here I was about to be filled with the semen of five men, and no protection.

I bucked my hips and pleaded with Jacob to stop. "Please... we need protection," I cried. "I'm not on the pill." I tried to move but the men pinned me to the bed, Jacob gripping my hips as he continued to pump wildly in and out of me. That is when I heard him groan and felt the heat of his come spray my insides. I shuddered and felt my heart pounding in my chest as my mind raced. What if one of them got me pregnant?

"You don't have to worry about getting knocked up if I fuck your mouth," one of the men said as I was tugged to my hands and knees.

I was maneuvered so quickly it was a blur. Almost instantly I was on my hands and knees, a cock thrust in my mouth, hands in my hair guiding my rhythm as I was being face fucked.

"Damn...Your mouth looks nice around my cock." I heard the man say as his bulging rod went so deep down my throat I gagged. "Oh, fuck yeah," he said obviously turned on my discomfort. He pulled at my hair, holding my head in place as his hips moved faster. He groaned as he fucked my mouth, quick and hard, as if it were a pussy.

I tried not to gag but it was difficult with a cock thrusting in and out of my throat. I made awful snorting sounds as I struggled to breathe, but that only encouraged him to fuck me harder. I felt the wetness of saliva dripping down my chin as I gasped for any air I could get. My eyes were watering as I suppressed my gag reflex as much as I could. Putting my hands on his hips I tried to push him away, but someone gripped me from behind and held my arms behind my back allowing the forceful mouth fucking to continue.

Fingers slipped inside my pussy. I felt my walls tighten around them. Was I really enjoying this? I wondered but only for a moment...The cock inside my mouth twitched and a hot load spurt down my throat. The man held me there as he continued to release his seed. "Swallow for me," he said, his dick still in my mouth.

His grip had not loosened and I had no choice. I closed my eyes, tears running down my cheeks, and swallowed the stranger's come.

His cock pulled from my mouth, I was pressed from behind face first into the mattress. "That was nice, Ben, but there is no way I'm not filling this pussy with my jizz," I heard Isaac say.

~

FACE MASHED INTO THE BED, arms pinned tightly behind me with my ass in the air, Isaac dipped his thumb in my pussy then pushed it in my asshole. Eyes wide with shock and terror I struggled in his grip. "No, no," he tutted as someone pulled the hair from my face and began rubbing the head of their cock on my lips. "Suck that dick while I fill you from behind."

I stopped fighting. My lips parting as I obediently suckled the head of the mystery cock. The thumb in my ass moved in and out, stretching my backdoor as the tip of Isaac's cock teased my dripping pussy slit.

Mentally I was still shocked and frightened, but physically, I was responding positively to the innumerable erotic sensations that now coursed through and over my body.

My tummy fluttered as hot rushes of desire coursed through my veins. My pussy twitched, eager for Isaac's cock as he continued to tease my hole with the thick head of his penis. "Mmm..." I moaned with a mouth full of cock and subconsciously arched my back.

"Damn, I do believe she wants you to fuck her," I heard Jacob say.

"I'll fuck her," Isaac said before thrusting the full length of his cock inside me.

I let out a muffled squeal as Isaac began pounding me from behind.

The man holding my hair continued to pump in and out of my mouth. I gasped for air, drooling down my chin, snorting as his cock forced its way down my throat. I felt his cock twitch and I braced for another wad of hot come in my mouth, but the man pulled out. "Oh no way. This load goes inside her ass," he groaned and mashed my face to the bed.

Isaac was still pumping furiously at my pussy, his thumb still wriggling in my ass. I squirmed as the heat of orgasm began to build up in my abdomen. Was I about to climax? I pushed the idea from my mind. What kind of a girl would climax as she was being brutally fucked by a stranger just to pay off her husband's debt? I shuddered as my body shunned my thoughts of purity. I was that kind of girl. The kind of girl who figured she should at least get something out of this experience. I clawed at the sheet as my pussy tightened around Isaac's manhood. "Oh God!" I cried out.

The men hooted and whistled as Isaac fucked me to orgasm. Then shortly after I came, he did. Gripping my hair, he pulled my long tresses back as if they were reigns, holding me tight as he mashed his hips to my buttocks, emptying his load, coating my insides with yet another dose of fertile semen.

With a smack on my ass, Isaac pulled out but before I could even catch my breath, two men grabbed me. Before I knew what was happening, I was laying on top of a man. He gnashed his teeth as he pushed me into position, his cock inside my still convulsing tunnel. "Oh, baby your pussy is hot and tight." He grinned, wrapped his arms around my waist, then pulled me flat on his chest.

"Get that booty," he said, and I felt the other man behind me.

I struggled against the man holding me to him. "No. I've never," I said my eyes wide with apprehension.

"Shh..." Jacob held my chin, squeezing my face roughly. "Andy and Clint are going to make you come so hard you'll never be satisfied by Burt again." He leaned down and kissed my mouth. "Relax," he said before letting me go.

I tried my best to relax but instinct was more difficult to subdue than I could ever imagine. I panted, eyes closed tight as hands caressed my ass cheeks and fingers dipped inside my buttonhole, all the while a thick, throbbing cock slowly slid back and forth in my pussy.

I could hear the man's breathing as he held me close to his body. Then I could hear his heartbeat. His arousal became contagious and I let out a soft sigh as my fears dissipated and carnal desire consumed me.

Once more I clawed at the bed. My thoughts a mixture of pleasure and guilt as strange men stoked flames of delight that I had no idea existed before this moment.

Suddenly, I felt the pressure of the tip of a cock at my anus. I immediately tensed up.

"Hold her steady, Andy," Clint said, and Andy instantly gripped me tighter, his cock stuffed inside my pussy.

I bit down on my bottom lip as Clint's mushroom shaped head penetrated my virgin buttonhole expecting to feel pain. The sensation was more like a fullness than pain as Clint slowly slipped a bit deeper inside my backside.

I felt my clit pressing against Andy's pelvic bone and my pussy ached then fluttered. I didn't know if my body could stand both of them inside me at once. Both Clint and Andy were rather well-endowed compared to other men I had been with before.

Just as I started to relax, Clint pushed his cock deeper sending a wave of sharp pain through me. I cried out as he forced his dick as far as he could, leaning on my back as Andy continued to pin me to his chest. The pain was sharp. I let out another cry and wanted to struggle but I feared more pain. But just as suddenly as it had hit, the pain vanished and I was washed in a warmth of pleasure like I had never felt before.

Andy remained deep inside me as Clint slowly fucked my ass. Both men grunted as Clint worked my asshole. The feelings were indescribably amazing. Hot tingles shooting from my ass to my pussy then spreading over my entire being.

Andy began slowly pumping my pussy shooting my pleasure levels over the top. It was only a few moments before another orgasm washed over me. My pussy tightened and maybe my asshole did too.

Both men let out an animalistic growl as they thrust faster. Clint gripped my ass cheeks kneading them as he shot the first load in my ass. In only a matter of seconds, Andy released his seed in my already sticky pussy.

I whimpered, trembling as come dripped from both orifices, overflowing with a mix of my juices and four men's jizz.

Weak with pleasure I rolled off Andy, lying in the center of the sweat and come soaked bed.

"And now for the grand finale," I heard Jacob say. "Put her on her knees, boys."

I felt hands pull me from the bed to the floor. I dropped to my knees as the men stood before me, cocks in hand.

"Suck it," Jacob said as he shoved his cock in my mouth. "Fuck yeah," he groaned as I choked on his fully engorged rod.

The men encircled me. Both hands now held stiff cocks while Jacob continued to fuck my mouth.

I heard the sounds of men groaning, felt dicks tapping along the cheeks of my face as they waited to plunge into my mouth.

The sexually charged atmosphere took over me. I found myself wiggling my hips, sex fluids dripping down my creamy thighs as I became obsessed with the urge to suck as much dick as I could.

"Mmmmm..." I moaned and pulled my mouth from Jacob's cock with a loud pop. I turned my head and took in the cock from my right hand. Suckling the head, licking the shaft, tasting the salty combination of my and the man's juices. Once more I pulled away with a loud pop and took the cock from my left hand in my mouth, pushing my mouth over the length until I made myself gag.

"Looks like we have created a sex monster, boys," I heard Jacob say. "Let's not let this little cock monster go away still wanting more." He chuckled and yanked my head back.

I looked up at him, eyes wide open, lips parted, tongue out.

"Mmm...that's nice," he said and tapped the head of his dick on my tongue before forcing my head over his cock until my nose was buried in his pubic hair. Struggling for air I placed my hands on his hips and tried to push away but my struggling only turned them on.

My hands were pulled from his hips as I gagged and snorted so Jacob could force his cock deeper still. That's when I felt it. His cock began twitching, Jacob let out a grunt and his come shot straight down my throat.

When he finished, he let me go. I dropped over, gasping for air, the room spinning, I tried not to pass out. After a moment I regained my composure. My pussy was hotter than it had ever been and I needed more cock.

Reaching out, I pulled the next cock to my mouth. Hungrily I sucked, licked and played with the man's balls. Without warning, he pulled from me and another man shoved his cock in my mouth. I lost track of who was fucking my mouth and who was pulling at my tits or smacking my behind. It was a blissful blur of pinching, tweaking, fingering, and sucking...something I never would have imagined I would be doing let alone, enjoying.

My hand wandered down to my pussy. I massaged my clit as cocks thrust in and out of my mouth, inching ever so close to my own climax. "Come on me," I whispered in between cocks. "Please...come on me."

"You heard the lady," Jacob said.

Everyone took a step back, cocks in hands. I stared in awe as they stroked their shafts and massaged the gooey tips of their dicks. By their breathing I was able to tell that it wouldn't be long before they would start to shoot their loads.

Eager to catch every last drop, I moved in closer, still

fingering my pussy, mouth wide open anxious for the first squirt of come.

"Fuck yeah," Isaac grunted as he held his cock over my mouth. I let out a whimper as the first rope of jizz shot across my face. With my tongue, I licked the edge of my mouth tasting his come.

Isaac was still dropping come on my face when another cock pressed along my left cheek. The first shot sprayed along my nose. I wiped it with my fingertip and pressed the hot goo into my mouth as more shots coated my lips, and that is when my orgasm hit me.

I let out a shrill cry. My fingers deep inside my semen-coated vagina, my palm pressed against my mound, massaging my clit, all the while men were coming on my face and tits.

I shook with intense pleasure, weak by my orgasm I nearly dropped to the floor but someone quickly grabbed me and held me up, so each man was able to spray his seed over my convulsing body.

As I shuddered on the floor, every muscle spasming. I knew I would be sore from all the abuse my body had endured...but I didn't care. I chuckled to myself, a smile curving my jizz-covered mouth. I licked my lips then ran my pussy soaked fingers along my tongue.

"What's so amusing?" Jacob asked as he stared down at me.

I squirmed, squeezing my thighs tight together. My clit was still swollen and sensitive, my pussy walls still quivering from orgasm. I looked up at the leader of the gang bang. "You were right," I said and chewed at my bottom lip as the hunger for more consumed me.

"About what?" Jacob had a shit-eating grin on his face as he watched me writhing on the floor before him.

"Burt," I laughed softly. "Hmmm, yeah, my husband will never be able to satisfy me again."

Jacob pulled me to my feet and pushed me to the bed. "Well we don't have to give you back until we feel fully compensated," Jacob said.

The heat inside me was nearly unbearable. I was not in the least scared of the men anymore. My pussy now ached for more and I longed to remain with them until the fire had been completely extinguished.

"So if you ask really nice I'll let you stay for another round." He smacked my left tit then tugged at my nipple. "But I warn you, we won't take it easy on you this time." He yanked my legs wide apart and shoved his cock inside me.

I bucked my hips to him, wrapped my arms around him, and clawed his back with my nails. "That's fine with me," I snarled before pulling myself up to him and biting his chest, causing him to let out a startled gasp. "I'm not interested in playing nice this time either."

THE END

GET ACCESS TO OVER 20 MORE FREE EROTICA DOWNLOADS AT SHAMELESS BOOK DEALS

Shameless Book Deals is a website that shamelessly brings you the very best erotica at the best prices from the best authors to your inbox every day. Sign up to our newsletter to get access to the daily deals and the Shameless Free Story Archive!

I'M NOT A BAD GIRL BY AMBER GRAY

There's nothing special about me. I'm just plain old Amy Rose. I major in accounting and go to church four nights a week. I don't dress flashy or go to parties or do much of anything.

I've never felt special.

Until Trey walked into my life. I've had crushes before, mostly the men on the old tv shows I watch with my family, but Trey was something else.

The tall and muscular dark-skinned quarterback thought that asking me to do nasty things would make me go away. Nope. I did whatever Trey wanted, even when he brought friends.

"That's enough. Y'all leave her alone," Trey said.

At the sound of his voice, the classroom went silent.

Trey never said much, but when he did people listened. I guess being a star athlete has its privileges.

Brandy Dean was petite and cute with blonde hair and almost green eyes. She was popular, and I was not. She had everything: money, clothes, and the attention of anyone who wanted to look at the cleavage she liked to display so much.

I had no idea why she couldn't enjoy her life instead of bullying me.

She'd been going on about my glasses, and as usual, I ignored it. I thought college would be different from high school.

I was wrong.

I waited for the next biting remark, but none came.

Brandy looked around the room. I could see from the look on her face that she wanted to say something to Trey. She had a few students who were on her side. There were three girls who hung on her every word and some boys who wanted to get in her pants. They were no help for her.

Then Brandy looked at Trey. I'm not sure if it was the fact that he was 6' 5" or the bandaged hand that stopped her. I didn't even like football, but I knew that Trey had hurt himself to beat a team we'd lost against for the last decade.

Brandy wasn't going to go against the campus hero, so she shut up.

Brandy shut up!

Trey wasn't even paying attention to any of this. He said what he had to say and then started taking notes. He was like a king who'd given orders and expected them to be obeyed.

The whole thing was amazing to me. I found myself laughing, almost giggling, and I couldn't stop.

And that is how I fell in love with Trey Le'vante West.

THAT NIGHT, I had a late dinner with my family.

We always ate late on Wednesday night. My father was a

deacon, and we were expected to be there. I sat in the same seat pew for the last twenty years.

At home, I quickly baked the bread and set the table. No sooner had we said prayer than my mother said, "You seem distracted, Amy. Is there a problem at school?"

We agreed that I could go to college as long as it didn't interfere with my home and church duties. My mother watched me like a barnyard owl following a mouse.

To be honest, I don't think she cared whether I went to college or not. I think she wanted to show my father that she was a good wife who raised a pious daughter.

"Um… There's some stuff in class that I don't understand," I said. "I just want to get it right."

If my father had asked me, I could have hinted at female problems, and he would have left me alone. My mother was not deflected so easily.

My mother said nothing but shook her head. She didn't have to tell me that she didn't think I was smart enough. My mother could speak volumes without saying a word.

"Maybe Bobby Reese could help you," my father said.

"That's an idea," I said in the most diplomatic tone that I could muster.

There was a time that I would've told him exactly what I thought Bobby Reese, a young man whose only ambition was to drive his pickup truck to deliver pizza.

Don't get me wrong. I respect hard work, but I didn't want to get stuck with a man who was happy driving around in circles all night.

Also, my father thought that any man was smarter than any woman. If I didn't understand something, Bobby could explain it to me. Well, Daddy, Bobby barely graduated high school.

So I bit my lip and ate my food and tried not to think about Trey.

~

I HAVE no idea what I expected, but the next class, everything went back to normal.

It was my first class of the day. I usually arrived on time. Except for that morning, I got in early.

Instead of my usual frumpy blouse, I wore something special.

A couple years ago, my family took in an exchange student. Her name was Anna. The plan was to slowly convert the Eastern European girl to our religion.

Anna had her own ideas.

She wasn't very religious or modest. She did agree with my father that a woman needed to marry young. They disagreed on how far the young lady should go in finding a husband.

She didn't last very long in our household. I will say that I learned a lot in the two weeks that she shared my bedroom.

She even left me some clothes to wear.

I was sitting in class, waiting on Trey, and wearing a color my father called Sin Red.

For maybe the first time in my life, I bared my shoulders and bra strap.

It probably doesn't sound like much, but it was a massive step for me.

Trey was one of the last to come through the door. As usual, he sat in the middle of the class. I sat at the desk to his right. I usually sat further towards the front. Again, it was a big step for me.

When Trey sat, I wanted to say something to him. A simple good morning would have worked, but I got a whiff of him. It wasn't cologne, but whatever it was made my brain freeze.

I made a sound like a cough that got his attention.

He looked up at me and did kind of a double-take.

From a couple of rows back, I heard Brandy say, "Someone's all dolled up."

Before I could say anything to her, Trey gave me a little smile and said, "Yeah, she looking aight."

Looking 'aight' was the nicest thing anyone's ever said about me.

That went on for weeks. Brandy would dig at me, and Trey came to my rescue like a knight in shining armor.

The funny thing is I could barely bring myself to talk to him. He was just so... big that I froze whenever he was around.

And worse, he could kill me with his brown eyes and crooked smile.

His hair was perfectly flat on top with the sides and back shaved clean. I wanted to see how smooth his skin was. As the weeks passed, I found myself thinking about him more.

I CAME HOME from class one evening to find Bobby waiting for me. He wore a brown suit and a green tie. It was the same suit he wore to church almost every Sunday.

"Bobby's come for supper," my mother said from the kitchen.

My father was sitting in his favorite chair, and Bobby sat on the couch. Bobby's face was flushed in embarrassment.

I wanted to slap the grin off his face.

I didn't know what Bobby and my father talked about before I entered the room, but I was certain that it wasn't good news for me.

Dinner that night was eye-opening.

For as long as I could remember, I did what my parents told me to do. I had three older sisters who had done the same. They all moved out of the house to get married to men chosen for them. They all had children.

If it occurred to any of them to get a degree, no one told me.

What I learned was that I had no choices. Married and raising children was all I had to look forward to.

What's worse is that everyone knew I didn't have a choice. I figured this out because Bobby didn't say much to me. He spoke mostly to my father because he was the person that had to be convinced.

IN THE NEXT CLASS, something happened to change my life.

Everyone was in a gloomy mood. It was like the joy had been stolen. Brandy and her friends were quiet, and even Trey was not his usual outgoing self. He was angry or disappointed. I couldn't tell which.

After class, I followed Trey out. It wasn't the first time that I'd done that. I followed him a lot, but I'm usually thirty to forty feet back.

"Trey?" I had to call his name repeatedly before he turned around.

Finally, he stopped at the edge of the parking lot.

"What do you want?" he asked me.

Any other day that tone from him would have sent me scurrying. I might have even cried a little, but not that day.

"I don't want anything," I said.

"Then why are you following me again?"

Okay, he knew that I was following him. I caught myself looking at his feet, but I had to remind myself that I didn't have to be shy my whole life. I forced myself to look him in the eye.

"I don't have a lot of friends," I said. "You were really nice to me, and I wanted to return the favor."

Trey just stared at me. The look was not cold or hateful. It was like I was some two-headed goat he paid a dollar to see at the county fair.

"What happened?" I asked.

Trey shook his head. It reminded me of a gesture my father used when he was frustrated. He turned and walked away.

I started walking toward my car when I heard, "You don't know, do you?"

I turned around to see that Trey had come back.

"Know what?"

Trey took a deep breath and said, "I threw three interceptions Saturday. We lost the game."

"Oh," I said.

Trey looked at me as if he were waiting for more of a response.

"Is that bad?" I asked.

At least I got him to laugh.

"Look, I don't know what to tell you," he said. "Brandy is a little bitch. You pop her in the mouth once she'll shut the fuck up and leave you alone. Not that complicated."

I stared at him with my mouth open.

I'd never talked to anyone that didn't see me as my parents saw me. I was sure that Trey wasn't joking, which meant that he could imagine me doing something like that.

"I thought you were in religious studies?" I asked him.

"So, I study religion. Don't mean I won't correct a fool."

I didn't have an answer for that. I felt like my brain was tripping over itself. Trey was crashing through everything I understood about myself. I felt like I was looking at everything for the first time.

He turned to walk away again, but I grabbed his arm. Trey looked at me like I was crazy.

His forearm was a thick band of muscles. I didn't realize how small my hands were. He could have easily pulled away, but he didn't.

"What do you want, Amy Rose?" he asked me.

That was the first time he used my name, and it felt nice in my ears.

I wanted to tell him about my father and my family. I wanted his advice about Bobby. I wanted to live my life, but I didn't want to disappoint my parents. How could I do it without hurting my father?

I couldn't tell him any of that. What I could do was offer to help him.

"You helped me," I said. "I wanted to return the favor."

I hugged his arm to my body. I immediately felt his arm between my breasts.

It was everything that I could do not to tell him that he was my lifeline.

"What? You crazy?"

I could only look up at him. I have no idea what my eyes told him, but whatever it was brought a smile to his face.

"You wanna help me so bad?"

I nodded.

"Then suck my dick," he said.

"What?" I asked. I wasn't sure I heard him right.

"Suck my dick," he said as casually as if he was talking about the weather.

I could feel my face flush. I looked around. If anyone heard him, I felt like I would die.

"I don't think... I..." I had no idea how to respond to that.

I let go of his arm.

Taking that for my answer, he walked away.

"WHAT DID YOU THINK OF HIM?" my mother asked.

"About who?" I asked. Her words pulled me out of my thoughts.

Mother sighed and spooned a small amount of mashed potatoes onto her plate.

She motioned to hand me the bowl but thought better of it. It was her subtle way of telling me that I was too fat.

"About Bobby," Mother said.

I was supposed to smile and blush, but I couldn't bring the strength to keep up the pretense.

"You want to die an old maid?" my father asked.

"I'm sorry," I said. "I have a paper due, and I'm not getting it right. My mind is there right now."

My parents looked at each other. I knew that wouldn't be the end of it. I knew I made a mistake that I'd have to pay for later.

I WAS SO angry that I didn't sit near Trey in the next class.

All I wanted to do was show my appreciation. Why did Trey have to ruin that? Why couldn't he just be nice to me?

I called after Trey a dozen times before he turned around. He looked at me with eyes that couldn't be bothered.

"You got something say to me?" Trey asked.

"Yes," I said with more defiance than I'd ever used in my life.

"What is it?" he asked.

My brain short-circuited again. I wanted to tell him how bad he made me feel. I wanted him to know that what he said wasn't very nice. But all the words got jammed inside me.

"You... I..." I choked on the words. "Fine, I'll do it."

The statement hung between us. I have no idea why I said it, and I had no idea why I'd want to do what he asked.

But, there it was.

He gave me a smile that no longer seemed so cute. "Do what?" he asked.

I felt my face flush. My feet wanted to run, but I forced them to stay in place.

"C'mon," he said.

I followed Trey like a puppy to his car. Trey opened the door for me, and I put my purse in the back seat.

"Where are we going?" I asked.

"Down to the lake," he said.

His car was nice. The white exterior seemed to glisten like pearls, and the dark leather interior was soft.

I couldn't tell you what songs he played. I wasn't familiar with the music. It was fast with heavy thumping. I caught every other phrase, include something like... bitch better have my money.

The lake wasn't far. We were there in a few minutes, and Trey pulled off the road and up a winding hill.

We parked at an overlook where a view of the trees, the lake, and the city had me almost giddy.

"You really gonna make me do this?" I asked.

Trey's answer was to unzip his pants. The zipper sounded impossibly loud. It had to be for me to hear it over the beating of my heart in my ears.

He pulled his pants to his knees. I saw blue patterned boxer shorts and something large underneath the fabric.

I shook my head. "I don't know," I said.

"Okay," he said. He pulled his pants up but didn't bother to zip them.

"That's it?" I asked as he started the car. Even I could hear the disappointment in my voice.

That bought a cynical laugh from him. "What? You think

I'ma beg you or chase you like I'm some hungry dog? You think you that fine?"

"What? Well, no," I said. He had me flustered again. Why couldn't he just talk to me like a normal person?

"Here's your problem. You want to do something, then do it. You a grown-ass woman. If you wanna suck dick, then suck some dick."

"But I don't want to suck dick!" I shouted.

What was Trey doing to me? He had me shouting and cursing. My parents would be so disappointed.

"Then why you out here? Why waste my time? I got classes too. You think you so fine that I'ma skip class for you?"

I shook my head. Maybe I wasn't fine. Why did he have to keep reminding me of that? My brown hair was nothing compared to Brandy. My breasts were small, and I wasn't petite. I wasn't even thin.

"You don't have to be mean to me," I said.

"How am I mean to you?" he asked. "I stood up for you. Everybody else make you think you can't choose nothing for yourself."

How did he know?

To the look on my face, he said, "You think you the only white girl dress like she going to church every day? You all the same. You want to get freaky, but you worried about what your daddy'll think."

I didn't like that he could see right through me. "I just wanted to do something nice for you."

"I know. You asked me, and this is it," Trey said. "You wanna bake me some cookies and shit? I can buy my own cookies. What I need is for you to suck this nut out."

I had thought about baking cookies.

"I don't know," I said.

Trey turned off the car. He pulled his pants and underwear down this time.

I wasn't completely ignorant. I know something about sex, but I had no idea how anyone would fit that thing inside her.

It was twice as long as I thought it would be. The tip was almost purple. I thought that it was supposed to be hard, but it lay on its side.

I felt Trey's hand on the back of my head. I didn't pull away.

"Open your mouth," Trey said.

I did. Trey pulled me lower until it slid between my lips. It didn't taste as bad as I thought that it would.

"Suck and lick on it," he said. "Watch the teeth."

His dick got harder, and I had more to deal with. He told me to use my hand to stroke it.

"Yeah, baby, just like that," he said.

I never had anyone talk to me like that. There was this tone in Trey's voice, a tone that excited me. He called me baby and told me I was doing a good job.

I was awkward and scraped him with my teeth, but we kept at it for almost an hour. Then, his voice got more urgent. "You ready?" he asked.

I didn't know what he was talking about, but I nodded. He gently pulled my head up and down. I could feel something building inside him; something was coming.

He grunted, and suddenly, I was tasting salty glue. I tried to pull away.

"Hey, hey, hey," Trey said. "Relax, girl. Hold it in your mouth."

I held it until he had me sit up.

"Let me see," he said.

I opened my mouth wide for him, showing him what I collected.

His smile warmed my heart. When he told me to swallow it, I gulped it down.

~

THAT WAS the first of many, many times.

The next time, I felt his hand slide up my blouse. All my upbringing told me that I was supposed to stop him. That same upbringing forbade me from being in the same car with him, much less taking his dick into my mouth.

When he pinched my nipple, I felt a shock run through my body. Then he circled my nipple with his finger. From that moment, whenever I was around him, my nipples would stand up.

It wasn't long before we moved to the back seat, where he pulled my skirt up and fingered me while I sucked his nut out.

Trey would drag me off for a "study" session at least twice a week for the next three months.

It wasn't long before I got our sessions down to fifteen minutes and finally, as little as five.

~

"I FORBID you to go to that school anymore," my father proclaimed at Thanksgiving dinner.

My parents, three grandparents, sisters, brothers-in-law, and a mother-in-law stopped eating to look at me. And of course, Bobby was there. I wouldn't be surprised if he had a ring in his pocket.

I am proud to say that I did not wither. I did not cry or beg.

"Of course," I said. "If I may ask, what is the problem?"

I half expected my father to bring up Trey. Truth be told,

it would almost be in relief. I felt guilty for sneaking around and lying by omission. I wasn't raised like that.

I wasn't surprised when my father went into a five-minute rant about the existence of dinosaurs and global warming.

I listened. I had the impression that my parents were small people, and I was learning to accept that. It was a suck dick or not moment.

"I was doing it for the family," I said. "The way I figure it, my sisters blessed us with these wonderful children, and I'll do the same. But, since they already have it done, I could be ready to bring in extra money if we ever need it."

"That's what your husband's for," my father said bitterly.

"Exactly," I said. "I'm here to support him. With a degree, I can give better support. I can help with emergency money and if you ever need anything in retirement."

I looked around the room, and most everyone was nodding. I could see that one of my sisters was jealous. I caught her eye and shook my head. She had to trust me to look out for her.

"It's accounting," I said. "So, at least we don't have to pay money to get our taxes done, and I could help with your store."

It never occurred to my father that any of his daughters could help with his business.

My father changed the subject to a different rant.

I let the matter go.

It wasn't until that moment I realized that Trey was telling me that I'd never be free until I broke away from the expectations.

I resolved to do something extra nice for him.

~

TREY WAS NOT in the next two classes.

Over the weekend, I found out that we lost a game, and that loss will keep us out of some bowl game.

Online, I looked at sports websites. I could see how everyone worshipped Trey at the beginning of the season. They talked about how he could be a professional. After the loss, all that changed. From what I read, everyone wondered if he could even tie his own shoes.

The pressure on him must have been awful. I knew little something about living up to the expectations of others.

I knew exactly what he needed.

"IS TREY HERE?" I asked.

The man looked at me like I was crazy. I couldn't describe him without using the word big. He had big hands and big arms and big shoulders. I was surprised that he didn't have to bend down when he went through doors.

"You here to see Trey?" he asked me.

I nodded and smiled as pleasantly as I could.

"And you here by yourself?" he asked me like I was a middle school student.

I nodded again and held up my basket in case he didn't see it.

"I baked cookies," I said.

"You baked cookies?" he asked.

"Chocolate chip."

He opened the door wide to let me in.

"Yo' Trey, you got a visitor," he said, stressing the last word.

"Bring them on back," Trey said.

I followed the man through a surprisingly well-kept

living room and a kitchen that looked like it should just be burned.

In the back, I found Trey and four others playing video games. Trey wore gray cotton shorts and a dark red shirt that was at least a size too small.

There were six of them. No one was shorter than six feet tall. I didn't realize how sheltered I was until I noticed that I'd never seen that many black men in one place.

"What you want, Amy Rose?" Trey asked.

He didn't look up from his game. I don't know what they were playing, but I could hear rapid gunfire from the large TV and speakers.

"I just wanted to see if you were okay," I said. "After the football game."

"The game's the game," he said. "We'll get that shit back, or we won't. I want to know what you want?" he asked me again.

"I brought cookies?" I held up the basket, and it was snatched from my hand.

Trey paused the game and looked at me. They all looked at me.

I wore a modest blue denim top and a floral-patterned white skirt that went almost to my calves. I wasn't showing any cleavage, but I still crossed my arms over my chest.

"What I tell you about bringing cookies?" Trey asked.

"That's not what you want," I said.

Trey grabbed a cushion from the back of the couch. He dropped it on the floor between his legs. "C'mon," he said.

"Here?" I asked.

"Aww, shit. This her?" one of them asked.

"Ain't that many white girls come over here with cookies," Trey answered, then to me, he said, "I ain't got all day."

I got the feeling that I could have left. No one would have

stopped me. Maybe that's why I got on my knees. I was free to do it or not.

Or maybe, he expected me to walk away with tears in my eyes. I wasn't the small person that Brandy could step on anymore.

All eyes were on me as I pulled Trey's shorts down to his ankles.

Every time I saw his dick, I was amazed at the size. I stroked it with my hand as the men made comments. I knew they were being lewd, but I felt like I was away from the words. Trey's dick was my universe at that moment.

I felt like I was standing on a diving board that was just too high. I guess that Trey sensed I needed a push.

Trey pointed his monster and shoved himself between my lips. The weeks we'd spent together barely prepared me for him that day. I let him use my mouth until my throat felt like I'd never swallow anything again. He didn't let up until I slapped at his thigh.

"Goddamn," someone said.

I was breathing hard, ready to go again, when Trey said, "C' mere."

He pulled me to my feet. Before I knew it, he'd pulled my panties down.

Everything I'd been taught about marriage and virginity went out the door as I climbed on top of him.

I didn't care who was looking or that they saw how hairy I was down there.

"Oh, God," I said as the head began to push into me. In fact, that's all I repeated for the eternity it took for Trey to stretch my poor body.

By the time he was halfway, I had sweat in my eyes, and my whole lower body felt like it was on fire; the pain was exquisite.

Trey looked into my eyes as he reached under my shirt.

Touching my nipples just the way I liked, I felt something build and release inside me. Soon, I was shaking from an orgasm, and Trey was all the way inside me.

Trey rolled me onto my back. I can't say he made love to me. It was too nasty for that. I can say that with a few minutes, I was shaking. It felt so good that I had tears in my eyes.

I'd learned how to sense when Trey was ready to finish. When he got close, I pulled him deeper inside me. I wanted him to plant his seed there.

I wanted it, and I didn't care what the consequences were.

When Trey ejaculated, I felt like a cup that had overflowed. I'd swallowed enough of him to know that I had a lot of seed inside me.

Wow.

I laid back and closed my eyes. I had no idea sex could be like that.

"You ever get your dick sucked by a white girl?" Trey asked someone.

"Yeah," a man answered.

"You ever get sucked by a white girl that do it right?"

"Naw."

I open my eyes when I felt someone crawl on the couch. The man was grinning and pointing a fat black dick at me. He was almost as long as Trey's manhood and just as thick. I took him into my mouth.

He tasted different.

Someone opened my legs and slipped inside me.

I had a hard time sucking with my body rocking, but we found a rhythm. Soon, I was swallowing more salty seed, and another took his place.

The next put his dick between my breasts. He teased my nipples as I sucked him. When he finished, I tried to catch it all in my mouth, but some ended up on my face.

I don't know how much I swallowed or who was between my legs before Trey wanted me again.

I was riding a huge bull of a man when I felt Trey behind me. He spread something cold into my behind.

I've never told Trey no, and I wasn't going to start then. I can't say I like it back there. I can say that I was thankful that he went slow.

When I came again, it wasn't so bad.

I woke up the next morning beside Trey in a bed.

My body ached when I moved, so I decided that I would sit still for a while. I let my mind wander as I thought about last night.

I couldn't help but grin. My family had no idea what I did last night with Trey and his friends. I felt free for the first time in my life.

I knew that I'd never go back to that shy person I was before, and that felt good.

THE END

GET ACCESS TO OVER 20 MORE FREE EROTICA DOWNLOADS AT SHAMELESS BOOK DEALS

Shameless Book Deals is a website that shamelessly brings you the very best erotica at the best prices from the best authors to your inbox every day. **Sign up to our newsletter** to get access to the daily deals and the Shameless Free Story Archive!

FIVE ROSES SOCIETY BY
CHARLOTTE STORM

Recent college grad, Jadin Haze, has big dreams and even bigger ambitions. Becoming a member of the posh and exclusive Five Roses Society would launch her career like nothing else. She's learned everything she can about the Roses. Everything except what happens during the initiation ritual.

All she knows is that five alumni have teamed up to prick her thorns and invade her bush. Now, she must hold her own against the older men and prove that even though her petals may be slightly bruised, no other Rose will taste as sweet.

*J*adin used the reflective windows on the limousine to make sure she looked the part. The instructions were clear. Her raven hair was to be twisted into a tight bun. She was allowed minimal makeup—lip gloss, blush, mascara, and eyeliner. Liquid eyeliner. Black. Her above-the-knee pencil skirt and low-cut blouse were to be tight-fitting and red.

Rose-colored red.

She didn't question the instruction. Not when they'd given a strict dress code for tonight and not when they'd insisted she stop taking any and all medications for a full month beforehand, including vitamins and birth control.

Any deviation in the instructions and her status as an initiate in the Five Roses Society would be revoked. There wasn't a person alive who could make her deviate.

Everyone who was anyone in her line of work was a Rose. Roses were kingmakers. Society-builders…and destroyers. She'd busted her ass in college, fucked all the right professors, and did more than her share of shady shit just to get the call to initiation. Jadin belonged here and there wasn't any length she wasn't willing to go to prove it.

That's how she knew she was ready. Pulling the puppet strings of the world wasn't for the faint of heart.

"Madam?" The chauffeur cleared his throat and proffered his hand toward the dimly lit walkway leading to the rose garden. Were she not so nervous, she would take her time, appreciate the estate, and the grounds that were well kept and world-famous.

Her first step scattered the butterflies in her belly. It felt strange not to have a handbag to clutch or even a cell phone to light her path. As instructed, Jadin had left everything in the limo.

Her pace was slow-going. The gravel was hell on her Louboutins. Those shoes had cost more than a month's salary from the job that had gotten her through college. She didn't care. She'd ruin a thousand pairs if she had to. Money wasn't something she'd ever worry about again if she passed the initiation and became a Rose.

When. When she passed. Failure wouldn't be entertained.

Finally, the wrought iron entrance into the rose garden came into view. A man dressed in a tuxedo greeted her. No, actually he didn't. He wouldn't look at her as she approached and definitely didn't greet her. He simply held out his hand. Laid across his palm was a black silk blindfold.

Tentatively, Jadin reached out and took it. "Do I put this on?" she asked, expecting an answer. The man did not respond.

What the fuck was she supposed to do now? She had no idea the layout of what she assumed was some sort of maze. Most rose gardens were. Was he going to guide her? How much help would he be if he wouldn't talk or even look at her?

Weighing her options, Jadin decided on practical and logical. She reached down, unfastened her high heels, and dropped them into the man's still open hand. "Here. Hold these."

If she was going to wander around blindfolded, she needed to feel the ground beneath her. Get in touch with her other senses. She'd get the shoes back later, she thought as she stared at the blindfold. Or maybe she wouldn't, depending on how the night went.

No. That was bullshit defeatist thinking her father had ingrained in her since birth. He'd wanted a son and Jadin had spent her youth proving she was better than any boy. Later, she spent her teen years trying to gain approval by spreading her legs for those same damn boys.

That changed the day she learned about the Five Roses Society from a history professor who wanted more from her than class participation and attendance. She never laid underneath those boys after that affair, preferring older, more experienced men. Men who could stimulate her mind just as much as her body. Men who could give what she craved most.

Knowledge. And with that knowledge, power.

She wouldn't get that power if she didn't pass tonight's

initiation ritual. And she couldn't pass hesitating at the entrance to her future. Steeling herself for whatever lay ahead, Jadin took a deep breath of the rose-perfumed air and placed the silk blindfold over her eyes. She made sure to tie it tightly so it wouldn't slip.

No slips tonight. Everything had to be perfect.

After the first few painful steps, the gravel gave way to smooth, cool pavement. Likely, it was marble. Roses spared no expense and, whenever they could, engaged in acts of indulgence—one of the five tenants.

With her hands out, one to the side, one to the front, Jadin made her way through the maze. She had no idea if she was going the right way or in circles, nor who was watching.

"You've made it to the first station, Initiate." The man's deep voice rumbled down her spine. She managed to suppress the startled squeak working its way up her throat but was unable to conceal the involuntary jerk of her reflexes. She silently prayed he hadn't noticed.

"Come, stand before me." Judging by the direction of his voice, the man was just to her right and slightly ahead. With as much poise as she could manage, she took a step away from the hedge that had been her guide and toward whatever task lay ahead.

She could sense when she was close enough to touch him. There was something electric about him, a current that made the hair on her arms stand on end. And his *voice*! She didn't need to see or touch him to know he had a strong physical presence and imposing physique.

"Jadin Haze…"

She shivered at the sound of her name on this man's lips. Though he was a stranger to her, she wanted him in a way she couldn't explain. Or maybe the reason why was obvious. This man had power. True power. Not the kind someone bragged about as proof.

"Do you vow to show fortitude where others would show uncertainty?"

Resisting the urge to squirm under what she imagined was this man's intense gaze, Jadin uttered the proper response, "I vow to do all that is required of me."

"Good," he replied, and she could hear the grin in his tone.

Just as Jadin mentally high-fived herself, she felt a hand on her shoulder which quickly worked its way up her neck to her cheek. This wasn't the same man who had spoken. His magnetism was different. So was his scent. He smelled like the air after a lightning storm.

"Do you vow to show courage where others would show cowardice?" Where Fortitude's voice had been strong and clear, Courage spoke barely above a whisper.

Jadin's response was automatic though she couldn't say for certain it was without a twinge of fear. "I vow to do all that is required of me."

"We'll see," Courage whispered even lower than before. Jadin had to strain to hear him.

Fortitude's thumb swiped over her lower lip, smearing her lip gloss. Her inner perfectionist cringed. She'd worked on her look for hours, taming every strand of hair, thickening every lash, applying and reapplying her lip gloss to find just the right shade of pink. The thought that these men would see her as less than perfect twisted her insides.

Her fingers twitched as her mind waged an inner war. Should she reach up and fix the smudge? Or leave it and let them—

Jadin's thoughts were ripped from her when Fortitude's lips crashed against hers. She held her own against his fierce advance, meeting force with force. From the sound of his voice, she had no doubt Fortitude was at least twenty years her senior. From the way his mouth and tongue moved over hers she knew he was far more experienced as well.

At the same time Fortitude assaulted her lips, Courage stripped her bare. It wasn't just the expensive blouse and pencil skirt he tore from her body that made her feel exposed. It was the way his hands intimately knew the weak spots in the fabric of her.

Jadin's already heightened senses burst with new life between these exciting and intense men. The two of them seemed to know when her mind drifted to the other as their touches and kisses intensified into a frenzied battle for her singular focus.

For a moment, Jadin had forgotten this was an initiation. That she was here for a different purpose than to be ravished, filled, and stretched by two strangers she couldn't see but never wanted to stop feeling.

Jadin was lost to them. Every time she breathed, it was Fortitude's exhale. Every moan was so Courage would know she was his. The lace of her panties rubbed her sensitive clit every time she bucked her hips. She was moments from exploding in ecstasy and all they'd done was touch and kiss her.

As if by some unspoken cue, both of the men stopped. Jadin's body screamed in protest. She was thankful she had enough fortitude to press her lips tightly together to prevent her displeasure from being known.

These men had teased her and she'd fallen for it.

"Mmm," Fortitude growled as he pulled his mouth from hers. "Strawberry. My favorite."

Her lips pulled into a smirk. It was her favorite flavor, too. Well, it had been until she tasted his lips. She wondered if Courage had a sweeter flavor. Head still reeling from her near-orgasm, Jadin felt as if she could float to the clouds. That was until Courage started speaking.

No. Not speaking. He didn't truly speak. He only whispered a string of complicated instructions which included where she was supposed to go next, codes intended to be spoken in a specific order, and secret hand movements only other members of the society would recognize.

Jadin found it difficult to concentrate with her still tingling lips and buzzing body. Both men had electrified her and the secret place inside her that wanted them both at the same time. She was insatiable in bed, so it made sense to have more than one man please her. That had been her fantasy, anyway. No man she dated yet wanted to invite others into the bedroom. It was an unfortunate circumstance she vowed to rectify.

"You may proceed, Initiate," both Fortitude and Courage said together. Jadin did as instructed, scrubbing from her mind and body as best she could her dissatisfaction that she hadn't finished with the two men.

The good news was that Jadin managed to follow the instructions given to her. The bad news was that it had taken her…well, she didn't know how long. She'd made a few missteps along the way and had to correct. She had no idea how that would affect her initiation.

Plus, she was chilled. Wearing nothing more than a blindfold and a matching lace bra and panty set, the night air kissed her exposed skin in a way that felt crude and unrefined compared to Fortitude's kiss. Maybe every kiss from now on would disappoint.

"You've reached the second checkpoint, Initiate." Honey dripped rich and sweet from whatever lips spoke. The liquid voice pooled between Jadin's thighs. The awareness of her orgasm denied rushed forward, demanding unwelcome attention.

The man's presence engulfed her even though he was, Jadin guessed, at least three feet away. Her mind turned to movies about fast cars, expensive hotels, and art collections. Her body warned her about the cost of expensive things. It wasn't about cash. Expensive things never were. It was about what she would pay to have the thing. Right now, the thing she wanted was to have a taste of this man.

A shiver rattled up Jadin's spine. Rattled, she thought, was the perfect way to describe her current state. She hoped the man would interpret her action as being chilled rather than weak and in desperate need of some relief.

"Do you vow to indulge in life's finer pleasures where others would practice moderation?"

"I vow to do all that is required of me," she answered back, hoping she would get to indulge in a good and proper fucking.

Indulgence took a step closer to Jadin. He smelled divine and dangerous—as if his scent were manufactured just for him by an exclusive perfumer only a Rose would have access to. His hand brushed her neck. There was that damned chill again.

"All?" His lips caressed her earlobe. The flood from earlier that hadn't quite dried soaked her panties. The dampness made the lace chafe her sensitive flesh. She wanted to beg Indulgence to remove them, have his way with her, take whatever was required.

She had no idea what made her want to submit to him. To the other men who'd teased her. Maybe the blindfold had been laced with Molly or something as equally potent. Or maybe it was that she'd never met a man she thought was worthy of that submission.

"All," she murmured with resoluteness he couldn't deny.

"Good." Indulgence grabbed a handful of Jadin's ass and bit her ear as he growled, "Because I plan on fucking your tight little asshole until you beg me to stop. But first, you have two more questions to answer."

On instinct, Jadin clenched her puckered hole and squeezed her cheeks together. "I don't beg," she wanted to say with all the strength and arrogance she'd brought with her in the limo, but the words died on her lips. Like her purse, phone, and shoes, she'd left that behind as well.

Besides, there was something wild, raw, and rude about a man with power over her future promising to use her body for his pleasure. She'd taken to calling herself a feminist since her sophomore year. Jadin now couldn't reconcile that philosophy with wanting to be taken and dominated by this man. By the three men she'd met so far. And by, she knew, the other two she was about to meet.

The Five Roses Society had five tenants: Fortitude, Courage, Indulgence, Adaptability, and Loyalty. And apparently the society was filled with sexy, older men Jadin craved. She knew the initiation would change her life. But she never expected it to broaden her sexual horizons.

"Be on your way, little flower. But before you go, these are mine." Without warning, Indulgence ripped Jadin's panties from her body. The lace dug into her before giving way under the destructive pressure. The sound of torn fabric and of Indulgence inhaling her scent shook all sense from her.

Jadin was moments from dropping onto her knees, unzipping his pants, and giving him no choice but to take her immediately when Indulgence smacked Jadin's ass. Hard.

"I said, be on your way."

Jadin's flesh stung more than her ego where he'd smacked her. The pain had made her grit her teeth. It also sent more need deep into her belly.

She tried her best not to stumble, not to look stupid in front of a man she couldn't see. She failed. That could be the only failure of the evening.

Finding the hedge, Jadin used it to guide herself forward.

Indulgence hadn't given her any direction and she hadn't dared ask for any. Her mind still raced with fear from her dissolving self-control, and from the promise he'd made to take her ass. No man had penetrated her there. She'd been determined that no one ever would.

Except, she'd also made a promise to do all that was required of her. If giving her virgin, untouched asshole to a man she craved was what was required, she wouldn't hesitate.

"Look at her," said an amused voice to Jadin's left. "It's as if she isn't even concentrating."

"Hmm," a lower, more serious voice answered. "I wonder what she's thinking about?"

Jadin silently cursed herself for being careless while simultaneously wiping her expression and holding her posture as straight as she could.

"Let's ask her," said the light-hearted voice that sounded too pleased with himself for Jadin's liking.

Instead of waiting for her to get to him, or beckoning her forward, the man's hurried footsteps told Jadin he was coming to her. Instead of stopping in front of her, the footsteps continued in a circle around her. She was ready for the question, had a response prepared even though it wasn't the truth.

There was no way she would admit the truth. How could she tell them she was nervous about being fucked up the ass by a stranger? That she had no experience in that area. That she wasn't sure how kind he'd be. How patient. Would he hurt her? Could she handle the trial? Was she really cut out to be a Rose?

"You know what I'm going to ask," he said as a statement, not a question. "You're thinking about how to answer. I can tell."

Jadin couldn't see it but she could feel him point at her.

She suddenly hated the disadvantage of being blindfolded. Of being naked and exposed save for her bra.

"I'm not," she said with more bite than she intended. Who the fuck was this asshole that he thought he could—

"You're lying." The man with the even voice had approached. Jadin hadn't heard him. She'd been distracted by...ugh, fuck. She really needed to keep her focus on the initiation and not on the game all five men were playing. This was clearly a tactic. A test.

Jadin opened her mouth to retort but the man who'd challenged her in the first place put his finger on her lips. "I would think very carefully before answering. My man, Loyalty, over there always knows when someone lies."

That was a trait Jadin herself possessed. A gift that had been hell on her relationships. No one needed to know the truth all the time.

"I don't doubt it," Jadin said, measuring her words. "But I haven't vowed not to lie to you yet."

The man Jadin deduced was Adaptability chuckled. "I like her. She's fun," he announced. To whom, Jadin wasn't sure.

Still blindfolded, she couldn't see her surroundings. All she could smell were the damned roses in the garden. The din of crickets made it difficult to make out what was happening around her in the background.

"I wonder..." Adaptability paused for what Jadin assumed was dramatic effect. "I wonder if she'll be as much fun when I tell her that the whole society is here to watch her initiation rite."

Jadin fought the instinct to clasp her hands in front of her in an attempt to cover her crotch. She'd never been particularly shy and she'd worked hard for the body she had. Still, it was a basic human instinct to protect yourself from the unknown. And yet, being a Rose was everything to her.

Hadn't she said already that she was willing to do all that was required of her?

"They're welcome to watch," Jadin said and meant it. Loyalty would know if she were lying, anyway. No point in doing that. Plus, she'd always considered herself a bit of an exhibitionist. "I will do whatever is required."

"But you don't know what the rite consists of." Now, Adaptability was just gloating. Even though he pushed Jadin's buttons, there was a certain charm in his wit.

"That's irrelevant," Jadin replied, then reaffirmed, "I will do whatever is required."

"She's telling the truth." Loyalty stepped in behind Jadin and put his warm hands on her hips. His breath heated the space just behind her ear when he said, "There's nothing sexier than a woman who tells the truth."

Ever so slowly, Loyalty's fingers traced up Jadin's spine to the clasp in her bra. He unfastened it and removed it in a way that gave her goosebumps when the fabric tickled her arms and nipples.

"I've got a truth for you." Adaptability crowded Jadin's space. One hand gripped her neatly made bun. The other her freshly exposed breast. "Your rite consists of the five of us ganging up on you."

He brought his finger and thumb to her nipple and squeezed. "We're going to use you."

He yanked at the bun until her hair came loose, ruining her hard work.

"We're going to push you."

He pulled out the pins that had held up her hair and let it cascade over her shoulders and down her back.

"We're going to fuck you. If you can survive the night with the five of us, then you just might have what it takes to become a Rose."

Jadin held her breath, unsure of what to do. How to

respond. Deep down, she wanted this. To be pleasured by more than one man at the same time. But she'd only ever done it in her mind. She had no idea how the real deal would go. If her stamina would hold.

Were all Rose initiations like this? And how would this work if she were a man? Maybe this was because, on her application, Jaden had circled Indulgence as the tenant she most identified with.

Good thing she was young and flexible. Jadin surmised that the vigor of the ritual was why the cutoff age for new initiate applicants was twenty-four. Legacy applicants born from a Rose had no cutoff age and likely didn't have to endure as harsh a trial.

"Do you vow to be Adaptable when others would be rigid?"

Releasing her breath, Jadin said the only thing she could. "I will do whatever is required."

Jadin braced herself, unsure of what was coming next. Loyalty, who was still behind her, tightened her blindfold. "The five of us are here now. Make sure this doesn't come off. If you see any of us during the rite, you won't be initiated."

Jadin nodded then adjusted the blindfold to make sure it was in place.

"I told you I was going to get your ass," Indulgence murmured from Jadin's right. He would, she knew. They would all get turns if that was what they desired. And she would let them as many times as it took to become a Rose.

Even if that dream didn't come true, at least one would—a thorough fucking by five more than capable men. Roses never half-assed anything.

Courage grabbed her hand and whispered, "Come." Jadin did as instructed and followed Courage a few paces before the grass of the garden gave way to carpet and the warmth of being indoors.

Maybe this was where the other members would watch.

The room had an earthy scent. Being this close to the garden, that made sense. It had another, stronger scent as well. Something Jadin knew well.

Leather.

The familiar fabric creaked when someone pulled on whatever contraption was before her. She reached out to touch it and felt the straps and metal buckles.

"It's a swing," said Fortitude. "It'll preserve your stamina."

Jadin nodded. She knew what a swing was. She'd seen the eye hook in the ceiling of her history professor's den. She'd moved on from him before she had the guts to ask about the swing she knew was meant to be hung from it.

The men helped her into it. Fortitude and Loyalty lifted her off the ground, though Jadin suspected Fortitude could've done it on his own. Adaptability strapped her into the basic seated swing position.

Now, all of her was exposed to the men and whomever watched. She was completely at their mercy, waiting, willing, and ready for whatever lay ahead. Her mouth went dry, but her pussy got wetter at the sound of expensive clothes, belts, and shoes being tossed to the ground.

Without warning, one of the men smacked her pussy then slid a finger through her wet. She jumped as much from the sound as she did from the shock of pain mixed with pleasure that rocketed to her toes.

Her lips started to swell as blood rushed into the injured flesh. Everything was tender and sensitive. "You want this," teased Adaptability. "You're ready for us."

"I am ready to do all this is required of me," was her automatic response. It helped to hide how nervous as fuck she was about the impending gangbang.

"I'm so ready to put that to the test," Indulgence challenged.

Jadin couldn't help but grin to herself. She was getting used to her men. She knew their scents, their voices, hell, even the vibrations of their auras…if there were such a thing. She didn't need to see their faces to know what was happening. In fact, the blindfold made everything better. It freed her to connect to the initiation and the men about to make her a Rose in a way she never had before.

Loyalty knelt beside her which meant she wasn't that high off the ground. Someone had tilted her position so she was now reclined, her head ever so slightly below her feet. "Did you follow the instructions about all medications and vitamin supplements?"

"Of course," Jadin replied, wondering why he'd asked her that now.

"That's true," he announced to her as much as to the others. "Well, then. Jadin Haze, do you vow your loyalty to the Five Roses Society, until your dying day, and upon pain of death?"

"I will do all that is required."

"Good." Loyalty stood and placed his hand on her belly. "Remember you said that after tonight is over."

Tears of affection welled in Jadin's eyes. She couldn't quite place the sentiment or why she was so emotional. Her period wasn't for another two weeks, and sex rarely made her feel vulnerable. But there was something about the way Loyalty touched her. Caressed her. It was as if she were something precious to him. Something to be cherished. She wasn't sure she'd ever felt that before.

Courage leaned over her. Not for the first time Jadin was grateful to have on the blindfold. He was so close his breath heated her lips and cheeks, bringing her mind back to the heat between her legs.

"It isn't fair Fortitude got to taste you earlier when I only got to touch." He leaned closer, his lips brushing against hers in a light tickle before his mouth fully claimed hers.

Fortitude made a grunting sound somewhere by her feet. "You can have those lips. I want these."

Jadin's gasp of pleasure from the thorough licking Fortitude gave was swallowed by Courage's hungry mouth. Being kissed and eaten out at the same time was a completely new sensation to her. Her mind didn't know where to focus. Her body wasn't sure what to do with the crossed signals.

It was overload. It was almost too much. It was pure indulgence.

Jadin sensed someone slide beneath her, heard the rasp of skin against the carpet. She knew it was Indulgence by the way he touched her ass.

Spreading her ass cheeks apart, Indulgence began to lick at her puckered hole as Fortitude slurped at her juicy pussy and Courage ravished her mouth. Her orgasm was sudden, wet, and violent. Jadin had no time to prepare, though what she could have done to temper it, she didn't know.

A cry of ecstatic relief broke her kiss with Courage. She couldn't help but spare a thought for her audience. Was she giving them the show they'd hoped for? Her body continued to spasm as her men refused to relent. God but they were going to bring her to the brink again.

Another moan of pleasure was muffled when a hard, thick cock entered Jadin's open mouth. His balls lightly slapped against her forehead because of the angle and the sway the swing provided.

His taste was salty and pungent on her tongue. She was about to guess who the cock belonged to when the man spoke, removing all doubt. "I thought Courage would never get out of the way. So many fun things to do with your mouth. It's so…versatile."

Adaptability groaned as he shoved deeper, almost gagging Jadin. But this wasn't her first rodeo. She knew she could take him all the way down her throat. Him and all the others.

While Jadin's mouth was being thoroughly used, her next hole was filled and stretched as well. It was impossible now to concentrate on her men's energy. To try and figure out the dance they weaved around and inside her body. And she supposed it didn't matter anyway. All of them would have her. All of them would claim her. All of them would make her theirs in their own special ways.

"That mouth is mine, next," Indulgence insisted, and damn. Jadin hadn't realized he'd stopped licking her asshole. They switched and Jadin's jaw needed a break, but she knew she wouldn't get one.

She could call mercy. She could quit. But that was never going to happen.

"Mmm, that's it," Indulgence moaned as he slid in and out of her mouth. His taste was sweet and rich. She'd dated an art professor briefly and this taste reminded her of him. Come to think of it, so had his voice.

What an odd thought to have, Jadin reasoned. Why would she think of a past fling now? Unless...

Jadin choked on the thought. Or maybe it was because Indulgence had shoved his cock too far down her throat. "You've got this, Initiate," he coaxed her, not once slowing his pace but, thankfully, shallowing the depth. "Don't give up now."

It *was* him. Jadin was certain of it. He always had a fetish for her ass. He'd threaten to take it like he had earlier in the maze and Jadin would always refuse him.

Son of a Rose! How many of these men with her right now did she actually know? How many of her past relationships were members of the coveted society?

Handling her gag reflex, Jadin did her best to pleasure the

man in her mouth while contracting her pelvic floor muscles for the man inside her pussy.

"Oh, fuck," Courage growled moments before he filled Jadin with his hot seed. She could feel his cock pulse inside her and knew the erratic strokes had to do with his orgasm.

Shit. His orgasm. He fucking came inside her. Panic rose just as hot and twice as fast as the man who probably just impregnated her. She was tilted down allowing the semen the benefit of gravity. And if she had four more men to take to the finish, she knew she couldn't clean herself any time soon.

Suddenly, Loyalty's words and gesture made sense. She was a vessel. Maybe part of becoming a Rose was creating a legacy. She was way too young to become a mother. Jadin wasn't sure she ever wanted to be one. But she'd vowed to do all that was required and she meant it. If creating a baby from this ritual was what was required, she would do it.

"It's time," Indulgence teased. Jadin's asshole instinctively puckered. She knew being too tight would make it hurt. She had to relax.

She took a deep breath and exhaled slowly. Just as she was about to take a second one, another man was inside her. "Damn, you're so warm," Adaptability said as he rocked into her, using the straps of the swing to pull her as far down onto his cock as possible.

God, he was so deep Jadin couldn't help but moan.

"How's your jaw?" Fortitude grumbled into her ear, using his strong fingers to massage the sore muscles.

"I'm good," Jadin assured him though the massage felt magnificent.

"I'm big," Fortitude admitted, not with conceit. He said it as if it were a pertinent fact Jadin needed to know. "You're going to have to open wider."

He entered her slowly, giving her time to adjust. He

wasn't wrong, he was huge. But the good news was that he was a distraction from two fingers being worked into her overly tight asshole. It burned and so did her jaw. That's where she chose to focus.

Eventually, with patience, both the fingers and Fortitude's massive cock glided in with ease. "She's ready," Jadin heard Indulgence say. She didn't catch all of the next sentence but she got the gist: Distract her.

Jadin sensed a man approaching her right side. It was either Courage or Loyalty. But when he softly caressed her hand and then brought it to his hard cock, she knew it was Loyalty. He was the only one who touched her like that and she liked it.

If I have to have a baby, I want it to be his.

The thought caught Jadin off guard. She clenched just as the swing was being lowered and Indulgence was entering her from behind. She almost choked on Fortitude's cock and squeezed Loyalty's dick too hard.

Fuck, she had to get it together. Calm her nerves. Make it through the damn night. Thinking sentimentally at this moment was a detriment. Maybe later, when and if she became a mother, she could afford sentiment. Right now, she had to adapt to her situation. Use her strengths to her advantage. Bring her men to orgasm and prove she could handle the rigors of being a Rose.

She breathed in through her nose, relaxed every muscle from jaw to ass, and let the swing hold her up. Her men did the rest. Adaptability and Indulgence created a rhythm designed to keep her full but not at the same time. Jadin wasn't stretched enough for that. Not yet, but she expected them to push it when the time was right.

"I knew this would be perfect," Indulgence grunted as he moved deeper inside the place no man had been before.

"So good," Adaptability hissed. Jadin imagined his jaw

clenched tight. She felt the sting of his fingers as they dug deeper into her hips. She felt the sway of the swing and the way his strokes had become erratic.

He was close. And from the way Indulgence moaned, he wasn't too far behind.

"Together," Adaptability grunted. Jadin assumed he spoke to Indulgence.

"Yeah," Indulgence ground out as they both pounded into her at the same time.

She felt bad for Loyalty and Fortitude. She hadn't been paying them any attention. She couldn't focus on anything except the sensation of being stretched as they both entered her at once.

Jadin's own orgasm rose to join theirs. She screamed as best she could with a huge cock in her mouth. Still, the vibration must've felt too good because a moment later, Fortitude threw out a few choice curse words before exploding down her throat. He was so far in she had no choice but to swallow every drop.

Jadin's body trembled with her spent pleasure as Indulgence and Adaptability withdrew. She'd never felt so empty. She'd never felt so alive. Her jaw had gone blissfully numb, a sensation she knew she'd pay for later when feeling returned.

Without warning, Fortitude bent down and kissed Jadin deep and hard. It was as if he was searching for something she'd hidden. "Greedy," he teased, licking her lips. "You swallowed it all."

"Come back for round two and I'll make sure to save some for you."

Fortitude chuckled. Jadin didn't understand what was so funny. "You know, little flower, that I'll be back for round two, three, four, and five."

Five rounds! How could she possibly last that long? How could they? Women were afforded the capability to come as much and as often as they desired. But even that had limits. Certainly men twice her age had similar limitations.

"Just because you haven't had any medication," teased Courage, "doesn't mean we haven't. Have courage, our little rose petal. We have until daybreak to break you."

"Not if I break you first." Jadin hadn't meant to say it aloud. But it was out there now. The challenge thrown. If they could work her, she could work them.

"Are you ready for me, Initiate?" Loyalty's voice soothed all her sore places. Places she knew would hate her in the morning.

For him, she could always be ready.

Loyalty took up position between her legs. But instead of forcing his way inside her, he took his time worshipping her body. His touch, featherlight, started at her lips and worked its way down her neck, across her chest, to one nipple and then the next giving proper adoration, then to her belly where he lingered just long enough to make Jadin think she was right.

They wanted a baby from her. *He* wanted her to have his baby. She couldn't explain how she knew, only that she did.

When his thumb slid against her clit, Jadin gasped. "Brothers," Loyalty said. Somehow, that was all he needed to say. They knew what he wanted, which had Jadin wonder how many times they had done this rite.

Everywhere Loyalty had touched on her body, the others now gave attention to. This was about making her feel good and not about their entitlement to her body.

Loyalty's thrusts were slow and deliberate. This truly was a ritual for him. Something sacred. Jadin believed that he must treat every initiate with this much respect.

With her five men worshipping her, Jadin was brought to five orgasms before Loyalty buried himself as far as he could and released his orgasm deep inside her.

When they were done, the swing was lowered and hot towels were given to the men in order to clean and soothe Jadin's weary body. She was given water and allowed to stretch her sore muscles all while the blindfold remained firmly in place.

Piped in through speakers from some unknown source, a bell chimed just once.

Round one was down. It was time for round two.

THE END

GET ACCESS TO OVER 20 MORE FREE EROTICA DOWNLOADS AT SHAMELESS BOOK DEALS

Shameless Book Deals is a website that shamelessly brings you the very best erotica at the best prices from the best authors to your inbox every day. Sign up to our newsletter to get access to the daily deals and the Shameless Free Story Archive!

SNOW WHITE AND THE SINFUL
SEVEN BY MARGOT DEVINE

Snow White's bodyguards, the Sinful Seven, have watched
over the Princess for years at the request of the Queen
Mother. She's insistent that Snow remains chaste, but when
you're surrounded by seven burly, muscled warriors all day
it's difficult to keep your thoughts in check.
Snow White insists on a visit to the local pub and it's there
that she sees all of her fantasies fulfilled as one-by-one her
reverse harem of champions conquers her in fine-style.
She's been pure until now, but Princess White is about to let
it all out—and in!

Snow White and The Sinful Seven often found
themselves the talk of the kingdom. The mysterious Princess kept her seven bodyguards around her like a
reverse harem. They had been assigned to her at first by her
Queen Mother, keen to keep Snow White chaste, but the
plan ended up backfiring enormously.

At first the Seven were duty-bound, but as the Princess

approached her twentieth year they found it increasingly difficult to stick to the task that they had been assigned, despite their handsome payment.

The longer they stayed in the Princess's charge the more she got to know them. Gradually she gave them each a nickname, having overheard their tales and exploits of years gone by.

Thrusty, Biggy, Tiny, Licky, Butty, Ropey and Mouthful. They were each their own person, but one thing that the Queen Mother had insisted on was that each man was a capable warrior.

What the Queen hadn't insisted on—and perhaps should have—was that the men should each be eunuchs. Had she thought ahead, the eventual consequences were avoidable. You can't surround a beautiful Princess with seven burly, mature men and not expect the fates to intervene.

"I should very much like to visit the pub," Snow White declared one day as she lounged in her private quarters.

"But madam, the pub is for the common folk," Biggy said. He was by far her favorite.

"Then I would like to see how the common folk live," she said.

"Can tell you a story of them, madam, if it suits," Ropey said from his spot at the tall window.

The Sinful Seven spent the majority of their day doing very little. On occasion Snow White would have them play hide-and-seek or pose for her as she painted, but many of the activities occurred inside—save for the odd playful jaunt with her horses.

"I know how all of your stories end, Ropey, you dirty bugger," Snow said, giving him a wry smile. Ropey blushed bashfully, but not bashfully enough to warrant a new moniker.

"How about another game of tiddlywinks?" Tiny offered hopefully.

Snow White got to her feet and moved to the resplendent mirror that watched on from the wall. "Mirror, mirror on the wall, who has the tiddliest wink of all?" she asked, trying not to laugh.

The down-trodden face of Tiny appeared in the mirror and the Princess looked back to him to laugh. He bowed his head, but secretly relished the Princess's humiliating treatment of him.

"No, it is decided," she declared. "Licky, prepare the horses."

Licky's tongue flailed around his lips as it so often did. He always kept them invitingly wet, waiting perhaps for the day when the Princess might allow him to perform the act for which he was most famous. Many a woman had been serviced at the tongue of Licky.

"Aww you thertain?" Mouthful asked. He was named not for the size of his endowment—unlike Biggy—but for his unfortunate collection of speech-impediments.

"I'm certain," the Princess said.

She walked to her window and looked to the oft-billowing chimney of the local haunt. The Cock and Bucket was regularly brimming with customers from all across the kingdom. It was the last place to get a drink on the way out of town, and the first place to get one on the way in.

"'Tis a dangerous place," Butty warned.

"I'll have you watching my back," the Princess said, bouncing her eyebrows.

"That you will, fair maiden," Butty replied. He had a certain *affinity* to a lady's posterior.

"Thrusty, go help Licky with the steeds," Snow commanded.

The pair of them scurried off in a hurry as the remaining of the seven tried to dissuade her.

"It's not the place for a Princess," Biggy said.

"I am nearing twenty," the Princess said, holding a soft hand to Biggy's cheek. "It's kind of you to protect me so, but I fear the time is nearing for me to spread my wings."

"A sad day indeed," Tiny said.

"Fear not. I cannot stay pure and chaste forever."

Ropey cleared his throat. He'd have another story to add to his collection for sure.

"It's decided, ma'am?" Butty asked.

"It's decided," she said with a royal nod.

Biggy put out his arm. "Then follow me, fair maiden."

Snow White and her harem descended from her chambers to the stable yard below. Each of her champions, save Biggy, mounted their horses, reserving the purest, whitest thoroughbred of all for Snow.

Biggy guided his Princess to the animal and dropped his knee. He enjoyed this part. He kept his face stoic as his six friends turned, each hopeful of a glance up the Princess's billowing skirt.

She put her dainty foot onto the knee of Biggy and then lunged upwards, tossing her leg over the steed and flashing her bloomers. Several of the men had to adjust their codpieces.

None had ever caught the sight of early-morning dew, however. The Princess often teased that she was panty-less, but so far no-one had confirmed it. The Seven liked to imagine it, regardless.

"Onwards, men," the Princess beamed, steeling her eyes on the path ahead and yanking at her horse's reigns. "Giddy-up!"

The Princess's horse lurched to life immediately, setting

off on a strong gallop that her bodyguards struggled to keep up with.

Biggy's horse was of good stock and despite its late start he was able to get out ahead of Snow and lead the way.

"'Tis the Princess!" a gritty urchin declared, pointing a dirty finger in her direction as she rode past.

"*Yaww* Princeth," Mouthful corrected.

The cool woodland air rushed over the bare flesh of White's face and shoulders and she sucked a deep breath, pushing her bosom into the bust of her dress.

"'Tis a fine afternoon," she cried ahead.

Biggy looked back, directing his eyes immediately to the bulging breasts of his would-be-lover.

"You brighten the day all by yourself," Biggy said.

The Princess looked to her favorite and twisted her mouth in a grin, noticing that Biggy was not yet meeting her gaze. His eyes instead lingered on the plunging cleavage that seemed to grow bigger by the day.

"Up here," she said, and his eyes finally met hers.

Biggy turned back to the path, ducking to avoid a branch before steadying his horse back in the center of the dirt-track.

"Not long now, ma'am," Ropey said from behind.

"I should like a mead," the Princess shouted.

The cantering thunder of the horses roared onwards, approaching the Cock and Bucket like a racing storm.

The thatched-roof of the pub came into view beyond the trees and Snow gave her horse one last kick-on.

It stretched ahead of Biggy who, panicking, dug his heels into the side of his steed. It bolted forwards until the two were in a race to the finish-line.

A pair of drunken revelers exited the pub as the cavalry arrived, sobering up to the daunting sight.

"'Tis the Princess!" one said groggily.

Tiny was quickly off his horse, bending over so that the Princess could use his back to dismount. She trod carefully onto him and he winced in joyous pain as her high heel dug in between his ribs.

"Princess Snow White," Biggy declared.

The two patrons applauded vigorously, knowing that an incorrect amount of vigor could see them beheaded.

Biggy stared daggers at the pair of them. He gave them a nod and they quickly took their leave, scurrying off down the pathway and into the forest.

"They seemed nice," the Princess said cheerily.

"Many more *nice* people inside," Ropey said.

Biggy opened the door and Thrusty burst over the threshold, quickly assessing the room.

"Ladies," he began, scanning the room to find none. "Gentlemen. The Princess: Snow White."

She swanned graciously into the room, seeming to float over the dirty, tiled floor beneath her. The patrons' jaws hit the floor in unison and the barkeep quickly set about polishing eight tankards.

The group applauded slowly, unsure now of how to behave. The previously raucous atmosphere had been replaced with one of unease and tension.

"A mead, good sir," Princess White said, approaching the bar. "Tell me your name."

"Polder, m'lady," he said, looking quickly from the eyes of Snow White and to the seven strapping men around her. There was not a smile amongst them.

"Polder, my good man!" Snow White said, slapping the wooden bar. "Get these fine gentlemen a drink."

"What'll it be, noble fellows?" Polder said, affecting an accent fancier than the one he was used to.

"Thixth ailth," Mouthful said.

Polder's brow furrowed in confusion. Thankfully Biggy

was on-hand. He raised up six fingers to Polder and the penny dropped.

"Six ales!" Polder said aloud. "Six ales! Of course! Please, have a seat."

The group turned round to notice the room was now decidedly empty. The last of the patrons scurried out through the door.

"Where did they all go?" the Princess asked.

Licky looked to the clock. "Their lunch-hour must be over, ma'am."

"Aye," Butty agreed. "Back to work for them all."

"Such noble work-ethic," the Princess smiled, falling for the ruse. Truthfully the whole kingdom knew better than to rub shoulders with royalty. It was just too risky.

The barman placed a tankard down in front of Snow. "Your mead, ma'am."

Snow White's blue eyes sparkled as she stared at the drink. She had never before tasted such nectar.

She took up the flagon with two hands and brought it to her lips, drinking it down heartily. Polder began to pour the ales, but his eyes were transfixed on the Princess—not only because of her beauty, but because he was eager to hear a lady review his concoction.

"'Tis a mysterious one," the Princess declared, holding the tankard aloft and studying it in the candlelight.

"The mystery becomes clearer on the seventh or ninth pint," the barkeep said.

Biggy shot him a look. There was no time for jokes here.

"A seat, fair maiden," Tiny said, offering the Princess the fanciest chair in the bar.

The Princess sauntered over, taking another sip of the mystery-juice and dropping into the barely cushioned seat.

She set down her drink and one-by-one the Sinful Seven

joined her, quietly sipping their ales as the Princess enjoyed a taste of normal life.

"Cozy, isn't it?" she said, bouncing her shoulders.

Biggy looked around the dingy bar. He hoped to God the Princess couldn't smell what he could smell. "You could say that," he said.

"Ropey," the Princess said. "Regale us with a tale."

"One of my naughty ones, ma'am?"

"Why else would I be asking?"

Everyone leaned in as Ropey began a story. He spoke of a down-trodden women of distant lands, keen to marry the Prince at his royal gala that year but battling against her sisters who each had their own designs.

He talked of glass slippers and dainty, well-to-do ladies; fairy Godmothers and spells; pumpkins and mice, and then finally he arrived at the good stuff.

None had ever heard the tale before. Each man's codpiece filled as the story unfolded, and Snow White came all a-fluster, her cheeks turning redder and redder as Ropey arrived at the climax of his sinful tale.

"The ladies pumped the life out of him," Ropey said proudly, delighting in the attention of his audience, "and Cinderella caught each and every drop all over her face."

"Every drop?" Snow asked, sipping some more of her mead as she sat entranced.

"Every drop, fair maiden. What she couldn't guzzle down she smothered across her face. She looked like a waxed apple, m'lady."

"Imagine that!" Snow said, slapping her thigh. "It sounds delightful."

Ropey scanned his eyes across his colleagues. Without even looking, he knew immediately that they were all in a state of 'salute.'

Snow White, whilst equally aroused, was much chattier. "I

didn't think he'd bed the three of them," she said, referencing the tale.

"A Prince can have his fill, ma'am," Ropey said.

"Can a Princess?" Snow said.

The men looked about each other, wondering which of them should answer.

"A Princess can have whatever her heart desires," Biggy said, much to the excitement of his compatriots.

"Then I should very much like my *fill*," she said mischievously.

If any of the Sinful Seven's erections had flagged, Snow White's sudden excitability was sure to see them return anew.

"Now, ma'am?" Ropey asked, his eyes widening.

"I see no better time."

It was the day that the Seven had waited patiently for. Each of them had wanted to bed the Princess, but knew that it was in direct conflict to their duties. They were bound to protect the Princess and do as she ordered, even if that order meant going against the very reason for their employ.

"Poldaww, lock the doorth," Mouthful shouted to the bar.

Polder looked up from his filthy magazine with yet another confused look across his face.

"The doors, Polder," Biggy said. "Lock them. And ensure you are on the other side when you do."

Snow White clapped her hands giddily. "An orgy!" she cried. "What fun!"

"You didn't hear that, Polder," Ropey said.

The landlord fumbled with his keychain, keen to leave before he heard or saw more that he shouldn't.

"I'll be back in an hour," he said.

"Or two," the Princess giggled.

Licky doused his lips with a fresh coat of saliva as the Princess's eyes scanned across her burly conquerors.

The door clapped shut and the lock turned noisily, trapping the Princess inside with her Sinful Seven. There was now no safer place for her in the entire kingdom and also no place more likely to see the Queen Mother's wishes laid waste.

"'Tis the end of us if we do this," Tiny whispered.

"Shut. Up," Thrusty said out of the corner of his mouth, nudging his meddling friend in the ribs.

"Who wants to be first?" Snow White said.

The men were chomping at the bit, but none of them wanted to be the one that broke the sacred vows. They'd have to wait for an explicit order—but they wouldn't have to wait for long.

"Licky," Snow said, addressing the luscious-lipped lothario.

"Ma'am?" he said. The men about him watched the exchange, enthralled.

"If you would be so bold as to entreat me to that delicious muscle of yours. I should very much like to see if the tales are true."

Licky looked sheepishly left and right, receiving a subtle nod from Biggy. "Here, ma'am? Now?"

"I would very much like that," Snow said.

She stood up from her chair and moved over to the bench at the far wall of the tavern. The men watched as she sat down on it, facing herself towards them. Gradually her knees opened wide and she reclined, opening her legs and lifting her skirt. The panty-less rumors were all-of-a-sudden laid to rest.

"Right here," the Princess said, and the men stared, mouths agape, as their lady patted the puffy flesh of her vagina.

Princess White's bloomers ran up her leg, billowing outwards, but the fabric was lost when it came to her crotch.

Instead it cut off at the top of her thigh, wrapping around her kempt garden and giving Licky all the access he needed.

"I've never seen one prettier," Lucky said, and of all the men there, he should know. He'd feasted on more pussies than a hungry hound in a cattery.

Snow White looked under her drooping eyelids at her conquerors as they watched on in amazement. Steadily she shifted her finger down along the groove of her pussy, relishing the sudden attention of the Sinful Seven. Before now they'd been solely responsible for her safety, but now they were being ordered to be responsible for her pleasure.

"What are you waiting for?" she asked. It was a good question.

The nervousness washed from Licky's face and he steeled his gaze on the delicious-looking target. His tongue washed around his lips again and he pushed back his chair as he rose to his feet.

He stalked forwards, his codpiece bulging. Princess White looked him up and down, lingering her gaze on the delicious packet that she hoped to claim soon in return.

"Treat your lady," she hushed.

He sank dutifully to his knees and stared ahead at her framed sex. "'Tis even better close-up," he said, turning back to his friends.

They stared on, silent. Each of them knew they were witnessing history. Ropey paid more attention than most, knowing that this might well be his ace-in-the-hole when it came to his collection of naughty tales.

Licky looked back to his fair lady. She stared to his mouth as his face approached between her legs. Her eyes closed as she felt his breath, and Licky paced it just right. He knew all about teasing a lady.

For a moment he waited—just long enough for Snow White's eyes to reopen and stare down in confusion. When she did, he lunged forwards, catching the Princess by surprise.

His mouth enveloped those royal lips of hers and he flashed his tongue up along her groove, tasting the sweet ambrosia of her pussy. It was the richest he'd ever had.

"Oh, Licky!" she cried, squeezing her shoulders together.

The men watched on as the Princess's breasts swelled with arousal, filling her dress close to bursting. Their friend's head worked busily, and out of sight the Princess's pussy eased out its juices.

"Come watch," Princess White said. "Come and watch how he pleases me."

The men stood up instantly, as though they had been waiting for permission. Each of them advanced on the act, looking down over the shoulder of Licky to see the union of his mouth on the Princess's pretty pussy.

"'Tis a sight, to be sure," Thrusty said, rubbing a hand along his cock. He could scarcely contain himself. No-one could.

"A thight indeed!" Mouthful declared.

The Princess moaned in her seat, looking across the chorus of bodyguards that watched on. She felt herself awaken sexually, as though Aphrodite herself had found a home inside her.

"Feast on me, Licky," she said, writhing and moaning before them all.

Her slender fingers came to the lace at her bust and she pulled it apart, unfastening her top so that her breasts started to spill out.

"Pull out my tits, Mouthful," she said. "Wrap that malfunctioning tongue of yours around them."

Mouthful moved forwards and the remaining men awaited their call patiently, their pants brimming with thick, hard cock—except Tiny, of course.

Mouthful fetched a hand inside her dress, relieving her breasts from their now unnecessary home. The men watched on as Snow White's big tits sprang upwards, her nipples already bolt stiff.

"The fruits of the Gods," Tiny said.

"And you shall remain hungry," Snow White giggled.

Tiny felt that very special pang of delicious humiliation strike his craw. The men laughed along.

Mouthful didn't laugh though. This was soon to be the high point of his storied life. "Delithiouth," he hushed.

With that he enveloped the royal teat, relishing the hiss of satisfaction that lurched from Snow's lungs as two of the Seven sent her to heaven.

The Princess focused on the fresh sensations that beset her. Her brow furrowed in pleasured anguish as the busy, unique tongues targeted her erogenous zones.

Between the joyous bursts of glee she focused too on what was to happen next. She wondered how sinful the whole occasion might become. So too did the onlookers.

By now her clitoris was as stiff as her nipples and a climax was a-brewing. Licky was a professional, of course, and the idea of not entreating his Princess to an orgasm never crossed his mind.

As such he feasted messily. The men watched on, making mental notes of his movements and style, should they ever need to win the heart of a lady. Licky had often said that the fastest way to endear oneself to a maiden was to give her an earth-shattering climax.

Snow White slapped a hand down on the chair and grunted hard. The men that fed on her each increased their pace, with Mouthful swirling his stumpy tongue about her taut nipples and Licky ravishing the stud of pleasure that peeked out from beneath its fleshy hood.

"Something is happening!" the Princess declared. In all of her nineteen years she had never experienced an orgasm.

The sensation possessed her, causing her body to convulse wildly. A series of moans, the likes of which no man had ever heard, leapt from the lungs of the writhing Princess.

The wooden walls of the Cock and Bucket rattled, and the watchful men's pupils fattened with lust. They knew they were witnessing a wonder of nature, akin to the legends of the green, northern skies or the whirling dervishes that spiraled through the Great Plains. It was something that few men would ever see and it would be up to Ropey to recount the tale accurately.

The Princess's chest flushed a red hue as the climax tore through her. Licky felt her pussy contract on his lips and he probed a tongue inside to feel the muscle within grip it. Her juices flowed freely, cascading outwards and sliding down over the equally virginal knot beneath.

Licky pulled back finally and wiped at his maw and the Princess seemed to return somewhat to earth, breathing hard so that her breasts pounded forth. Mouthful pulled away too, wondering if perhaps the Princess was finished. Not by a long shot.

"Don't just stand there, Biggy," Snow White said, looking to her favorite champion. "Take out the thing that's filling your pantaloons and give us all a show."

Biggy paused for but a moment and then carried out the lady's request. His muscled arm reached forwards and down into his pants and now it was Snow White's turn to be enraptured.

She had heard the tales—and had given him the nickname —but she had never witnessed the thickness. It did not disappoint.

Biggy pulled himself over the waist of his pants to the

sound of several gasps. Princess Snow White was the most surprised of all.

"It's so big!" she swooned. "It seems unnatural."

"I'm afraid it is all natural," Biggy said, and he bounced the huge cock against his palm.

A thick vein ran up its exterior, breathing life into the appendage. Gradually it grew further, stiffening up against his open hand under the watchful eye of the salivating Princess.

"I want it," she said. "I want it oh-so desperately."

"Have it, my lady," Biggy said.

Snow White lurched forward and took up his cock in her soft grip. She felt along it, rejoicing in the bursts of blood that she sensed against her skin.

"It's *throbbing*," she cried, looking to Biggy.

"It does that," he said.

Her hand moved slowly along it, looking up to see if she was doing everything correctly. "Is that good?" she asked, making sure.

"The touch of your graciousness is always divine, my lady," Biggy said.

He closed his eyes and sighed as Princess White pumped slowly down the barrel of his flesh. Her pussy salivated wildly and so too did her mouth.

Steadily she leaned her head forwards and the six men around her moved in closer. Tiny rubbed a hand over the nub that was his cock as Thrusty started to buck back and forth, as though he was committing the act himself.

"Thwallow him, m'lady," Mouthful urged.

"I'll try," she chuckled, but turned serious soon enough.

She opened her mouth wide and spread it over the bulbous, delicious crown of her favorite fellow. Biggy sighed. It had been a long time since a lady had done that to him, especially one so fair as Princess White.

The Princess pushed onwards until she could claim no more of him. Six or seven inches remained unclaimed, but the Princess used both her hands to fill the vacant spot. She rolled them down and bobbed her head, delighting Biggy as she treated him to her drooling mouth.

"I want you all out of your pants, right now," she said quickly. "Except for you, Tiny."

Tiny knew his place. He was content to watch from the sidelines, knowing that he had nothing to offer his Princess apart from his skills with a sword.

Butty was the next to reveal himself. Snow White watched as he tugged his cock free, then turned along the chorus line and watched every other stiff cock become revealed. She had never before seen one phallus, and now she was casting her eyes across six well-endowed men, each sporting the stiffest erection that they'd ever known.

"Jerk them for me, boys," she urged, returning to Biggy's cock.

She sucked along him, wetting up his pole so that the tunnel of her hands and mouth was slick and warm. Biggy's balls fattened, filling with a volley of spunk that Ropey would be proud of.

"All of you," she said, looking across them. "I want you all."

The men moved closer until they had surrounded her in a semi-circle. Tiny stood on the outside, vying for an angle that he could capture the sin from.

Snow White pulled Biggy from her lips, kissing him goodbye before moving along down the line. Thrusty, Licky, Butty, Ropey and Mouthful all received their treats in turn. With each cock that she tasted the Princess tried to reach her lips further down, eventually discovering that a gag-reflex was something she didn't possess.

Mouthful was the proud recipient of her throat. He stared

down in amazement as his entire cock disappeared inside the mouth of the Princess. His friends stared in bewilderment, looking to Mouthful and then to the Princess, thinking them complicit in some kind of magic trick.

"He's in her throat!" Ropey declared.

"Impossible!" Butty said.

The Princess was keen to show them. She pulled back slowly, unsheathing the thickness from her. It re-emerged, wet with the thick saliva from her throat and as thick as ever.

"Wow!" Licky gasped.

"It feelth incwedible!" Mouthful called. Tiny could only imagine.

"Again," Biggy said, and now it was the Princess's turn to be dutiful.

She ran back along the chorus-line of cocks, surging each one deep and giving them a taste of her tight throat before arriving to Biggy once more.

"Don't worry, my Princess," he said, holding her face. "I'll take what I can get."

As much as the Princess wanted Biggy in her gullet she knew it would be impossible. "I have a greater treat for you yet," she said.

"M'lady?" Biggy inquired.

"You can be the first," she said.

"The first to what?" he asked.

"The first to come inside me."

With that the Princess pushed Biggy into her mouth, covering a smidgen more of his cock with her lips than before.

Biggy's enjoyment was heightened, not just by the extra inch of mouth-cover, but by the thought of taking the chastity of the devilish damsel.

"She plans to fuck him," Ropey gasped.

"I don't think she *just* wants him," Thrusty said, still bucking at the hips.

She peeled her lips back over Biggy's cock and addressed their suspicions. "I want you all," she said. "I want all of your cum."

By now Tiny wasn't even worthy of address, but the remainder of the Seven felt their hearts skip a beat.

Snow White could feel the adrenaline surging through her too. She'd had the thought, but her announcement of it had made the whole thing real. She felt a pang of danger and excitement at being filled by the experienced conquerors. They'd had many women in their time, but she doubted they'd ever shared one woman so freely.

"I want you," she said to Biggy now, and she fell back to her place on the bench.

"You don't need to tell me twice, ma'am," he said.

All but Tiny started to undress, showing off their chiseled physiques and battle-scarred bodies. The Princess loosened her dress and stepped out of it entirely, standing proud in the crotchless one-piece that struggled to cover her modesty. Her full breasts hung out from the top and her perfectly trimmed pussy sat on show beneath.

She sat back in the chair and opened her hips wide. "Slide it in," she dared.

Biggy received several pats across his broad back as he stepped forwards dutifully. He jerked back along his cock and brought the swelling head to the tightness of his Princess. It looked like an equation with no solution, but when he started to push against that virginal muscle of hers he found that it opened steadily.

"Yes!" cried Princess White.

Biggy often found his women tight due to the nature of his cock, but he never found them as tight as the Princess.

She gripped him like his own skin, squeezing snuggly around every inch that he pushed forcibly deep.

"Give it to her," Ropey goaded, and seven sets of eyes watched the deflowering closely.

The bulbous tip of Biggy sprouted through the tight aperture and Snow White let out a wail of delight as she took her conqueror.

Another inch burst forth, glossed by the juices that Licky had coaxed free. They smothered Biggy and eased his passing, allowing yet another inch of his dick to enter the fair maiden. Such was his size that her stomach bulged.

"Yes!" she whimpered, feeling the full, painful burst. "I am undone!"

"You are, my lady," Biggy said calmly, trying desperately to hide his joy.

"Good girl," Thrusty said, imagining himself buried within his Princess.

Biggy was deep within her now and slowly he started to fuck her, being gentle and paying close heed to her whimpers. But Snow White wasn't done. She wanted more.

"Thrusty," she said breathless, and the bucking bodyguard looked to her in anticipation.

"Yes, m'lady?" he said.

"In my mouth. Now."

Thrusty swallowed and stepped forwards, mounting the bench and angling his rod towards Snow's waiting mouth.

She looked to the approaching length and as it swung in her direction she took it in her grasp. Biggy slid himself through her and the Princess breathed fast, trembling all over. Her lips parted and Thrusty popped himself inside, relaxing into her warmth like a hot bath after a hard day.

Snow's head rocked over the second phallus, popping him almost free before sliding her plump lips back down over Thrusty.

"Yes," Licky said slowly.

The remaining four jerked themselves slowly, proud to be a witness to it all but keen too to be involved.

Snow yanked the hard cock from her maw. "Fuck my mouth, Thrusty, I know you can do better than that."

She placed her lips back over him and Thrusty became unleashed. With the Princess's permission granted he started to lunge into her, passing his cock right past her gullet so that her throat bulged along with her stomach.

Biggy pumped hard and Thrusty pumped too, both men heading towards an inevitable climax. There was nothing more intoxicating to any of them. They'd all had the fair share, of course, but none of them had ever bedded a Princess.

Ropey held one hand to his chin and watched, mesmerized by his friend's style. They each knew—or had been told—of the conquests of their colleagues, but none had ever really witnessed them in action.

"Good job, Thrusty," Ropey said, nodding in approval.

Thrusty didn't respond. Instead his eyes were steadfast on his Princess, looking down to her pure, serene face as his cock filled it over and over.

"I'm close m'lady," Thrusty said. No man could blame him.

Princess Snow hummed in approval, moving her head faster to meet his thrusts. Her eyes welled with her efforts and then they bulged as Thrusty groaned loud.

"Yes, my Princess!" he cried, and every man to the last knew what it meant.

For the moment Biggy tempered his movements, giving the Princess the opportunity to deal with the flood of cum that was now pouring into her throat.

She swallowed gleefully and then pulled back, releasing

the intruder from her neck before beating the shaft and lapping up the remaining lashes.

"You too now, Biggy," she said. "Come inside me."

Biggy took a grip of the Princess' thigh. She wiped at her mouth and looked down, watching the hilt of her man disappear and feeling herself become impossibly full. The satisfaction of Biggy's girth was immeasurable. She felt complete.

"Licky," she cried. "You now."

She beckoned him with a finger, but truthfully the Princess could scarcely muster an instruction. The pace and sensation of Biggy's stabbing cock was more than enough to occupy her.

"Oh, my Princess," Biggy groaned.

"Good boy," Princess White hushed. "Good boy. Come inside me. Come inside me."

Licky approached and the Princess snatched up his cock, putting it in her mouth in an instant. He could feel the velvet slipperiness of Thrusty within her still. It mingled with her spit and she slid her lips over it fast. The whole thing was hotter than hell.

By now Biggy was a sweat-dappled mess of ecstasy. He could feel the orgasms tingling in his weighty balls as they slapped heartily against the Princess's ass beneath. Eventually they pulled tight to his shaft, keen to deliver their deposit.

"It's here," he announced.

"Good!" the Princess cried. "Now shoot it up me!"

Biggy let out a warrior's cry and then throbbed into his mistress, letting out rope after thick rope. Each pulse from his cock was evident. Snow's stomach would ripple and Biggy would let out a loud cry, firing off the jets of his warm love that were embraced by Snow White gladly.

"Yes! Every drop! Be a good boy! Give me every last drop!"

For now Licky waited, watching as his friend emptied within Princess White.

"Good boy!" Snow White said, breathless, and then she latched herself onto Licky and continued working his cock.

Butty, Mouthful and Ropey stood around the Princess watching close, with Tiny off in the corner, peering through the bodies and hoping for a glimpse.

A bead of Biggy's enormous deposit announced itself at the core of Princess White, and she moved a hand to slather it back up her pussy before pushing a finger inside. She hummed contently at the warmth, but it was not enough for her.

"Butty," she said quickly. "On your back."

Butty looked down to the dirty tiled floor but paid it no mind. He'd have lain down in shit if it meant he could fuck the Princess.

"Like this, m'lady?" Butty said.

The Princess glanced down to her buff warrior as he held his cock upright, lying supine on the cool, hard floor.

"Exactly like that," she smirked, and she sank a finger into her garden again. This time she rubbed the cum-soaked digit down over her forbidden knot and Butty's eyes sparkled.

"I want you in my ass," she said.

Butty's cock was thinner than the rest and she could think of no better place for it. Besides, she knew it was the only place he'd want to stuff her.

Princess White was acting very unladylike, but her harem was not complaining. Instead, they were watching as the Princess stuffed two of her digits in her back-passage before slipping Licky back in her mouth.

She sucked for a moment longer as Butty continued to prime himself on the floor. There was no danger of his stiffness failing, but his shoulders were beginning to ache.

"Now," she said, sliding forward off the bench. "Let's see about that cock in my ass."

Butty smiled wider than anyone ever had in the entire kingdom. He watched his dainty Princess wander over, her pussy a sticky, glossed mess.

She faced her ass to Butty's head and bent down, affording him a look at the sinful dot of an asshole that looked for all the world inaccessible.

"Get him in you, m'lady," Ropey encouraged.

Princess White dropped slowly, angling her ass towards the waiting column. Butty's taut head pressed against the cum-glossed asshole and popped through the twangy muscle.

"Yes," Princess White hushed.

She sank slowly and Butty watched his inches disappear inside. The warmth of her ass felt pleasant around him. Her muscle hugged him close.

"Easy," Princess White laughed.

She reclined back against Butty and he felt her weight on his chest. The hard floor beneath turned more uncomfortable still, but Butty didn't care. It was a minor sacrifice.

"Licky," she said, and he knew what to do.

He moved back to her mouth and the Princess used a hand to prop herself upright, slipping the appendage back inside her and picking up where she'd left off.

"Ropey," she said, and she pointed a finger down at the floor to her left, opposite Licky.

Ropey joined his friend at the head of the Princess and she welcomed him by slipping his cock into her mouth and sucking deep.

"Joyous joy," Ropey whimpered.

Mouthful watched on, joined by Biggy whose erection was beginning anew. Thrusty still had work to do.

The Princess bounced steadily, grinding her ass down on

Butty's stiffness and sending him deep into her nethers. But still, it was not enough.

"Mouthful," she said.

"M'lady?"

Princess Snow patted between her legs at her sticky pussy. "In here. Now."

Mouthful stared at the wet, soft-pink opening. Beneath it Butty's cock squirmed, the strong muscle buried deep in the wrong hole.

"Wight you aww," Mouthful said.

He knelt astride the straight legs of Butty and held the hilt of his cock, washing it back and forth across the Princess's slippery pussy.

"Magnifithent," he whispered.

Mouthful pushed forwards and was hugged immediately by the warm, wet, sticky embrace of his Princess's royal petals. It felt divine.

"My cock hath nevaw been tweated to thutch plethyaw."

The Princess stifled a giggle and as she did so her muscles tightened. Mouthful and Butty both groaned, feeling the brief grip of their maiden about the girths.

"Now power-fuck me, boys," the Princess ordered.

Butty led the charge, thrusting up from the floor so that the Princess started to bounce. Her heavenly tits wobbled on her chest, spinning above her one-piece underwear.

Biggy watched, jerking steadily as the cocks of his companions speared the Princess one-by-one.

Ropey jerked steadily while Licky enjoyed the Princess's mouth, then the two would switch roles when her head turned in the opposite direction.

Mouthful was bouncing forward into his Princess, his face serene as though he was floating in the rivers of Elysium itself.

"Give me your cum boys," she urged. "I want it all."

The Princess writhed amongst the throngs of bodies, doling out the eternal pleasure within her. So long had she remained chaste that she had stored up enough sin to satisfy six men at once—which was just as well. She held a special pleasure too for the knowledge of how mortified the Queen Mother would be when she found out.

Butty was the first to seize up. His legs straightened and his toes curled as the Princess jerked him in her virginal asshole.

"My lady!" he groaned.

"Yes, Butty," she said. "Give it me!"

Her yearning was so strong that Butty could not deny her. His cock twitched in its favorite spot and soon arcs of his love were firing up into his lady's bottom.

"My gosh!" she cried. "It feels so funny!"

"It will!" Butty groaned, an expert. "But fear not!"

He pumped upwards, passing his cock through the slipperiness of Princess White's cum-sodden passage and adding to it all the while. More and more of his hot ropes leapt forth until he had given her everything.

Mouthful's lip began to curl now.

"Are you close?" the Princess asked, her eyes like raging whirlpools of excitement.

"I have appwoached!" Mouthful declared.

His eyes closed and the Princess felt him throb, adding his deposit to Biggy's before him. Their cum mingled within her and the increasing danger of pregnancy loomed large in her craw. It was hot to think about. There'd be no greater gut-punch to the Queen Mother than a newborn royal.

Butty stayed within his Princess, safe in the knowledge that any baby would not belong to him. His cock remained bolt stiff, and who could blame it. Of all the assholes in the kingdom, this was the pinnacle.

Mouthful continued his release, shrieking out barely intelligible sentences that caused the other men to laugh.

"T'ith like a thouthand dawnth!" he groaned, looking down as he pulled back and pinched out the final few beads of his love.

His cock emerged all slippery, squirming free and being quickly taken up in his hand. He gave himself some after-care, jerking softly as he looked down on the fair maiden below him, who looked at her least 'fair.'

"Now you, Licky," she groaned, and she stuffed him into her mouth and jerked him fast.

Ropey jerked too, watching the Princess's face and relishing the thought of covering it in his cum. Of the seven of them, Ropey was known to have the most bounteous release.

"Do not leave my pussy empty," the Princess was able to say in a brief pause of ferocious sucking.

Thrusty looked to Biggy. Only one of them was ready to go again.

Biggy stepped forwards and knelt to the floor, ready again to fill up his Princess. He sank inside the warm, slick hole and let out another satisfied sigh. Fucking the Princess was prize enough, but fucking her twice in on session? Well that was just divine.

Licky was breathless. His head was cast back, gasping, and the Princess was sucking him eagerly with a vibrancy of youth. The Sinful Seven knew from experience that the Princess was a bundle of energy, and now they were finding out in the most fantastic way possible.

"My turn," Licky cried, and the Princess's cheeks filled with the first blast of his love.

He looked down to see Snow White driving him deep, unabashed by the sudden influx of cum in her mouth.

Licky groaned and groaned, emptying more and more of

himself inside the Princess. Biggy watched on, beginning his rhythm anew and realizing immediately that he would not have the same staying-power as before.

As if to tempt it from Biggy faster Ropey suddenly let out a cry. The Princess barely had time to turn her head and soon Biggy was watching as the love poured out from Ropey's cock. Every person in the room soon realized the reason for his nickname.

The Princess gasped breathlessly, finding only the pearly release of Ropey instead of the air she craved. His hefty lashings blasted over her, lacing her face in a latticework of cum that the crown's baker would be proud of.

Ropey made a real show of it. He grunted and groaned, lurching his hand and tossing his muck far and wide. It dribbled down off the Princess's chin and coated her royal charms too.

"What a shot!" Princess White laughed, blinking through the cum that had webbed across her lashes.

Ropey wiped it away tenderly with a thumb as the Princess slowly bounced on the hard cock of Butty that sat up inside her.

Biggy was breathing hard too now and the Princess noticed his second-coming.

"Again so soon?" she said wryly.

"My apologies," Biggy croaked.

"Do not apologize," the Princess said sincerely. "Or if you do, apologize by shooting another lashing inside me."

Biggy did just that. No sooner had she demanded it, Biggy's cock was firing another volley of spunk deep inside her already full core.

It flowed into her and Biggy pushed deep, displacing the pool of cum that was already inside her. Butty felt it roll down out of her and onto his coin-purse.

"Good boy," Princess White said, holding Biggy's face and staring into his eyes. "If I have a child, I'd want it to be yours."

It was no revelation. The remaining six always knew that Biggy was her favorite. It made sense. He was more alpha-male than all of them.

She reached her head forwards and kissed tenderly at Biggy's quivering lip. The last of him flowed into her and the kiss blossomed sensually. Were it not for the cock in Princess White's ass and the crowd of onlookers, one might even call the kiss 'romantic.'

Snow White rolled her tongue over her teeth and bit her lip. Biggy eased out of her and another flow of white cream ran forth.

She grunted and lifted herself slowly off of Butty, affording him one last slow jerk from her tight, forbidden hole.

He popped free and sat up, rubbing at his lower-back, but caring little for what ailed it. He'd already been given ample compensation for any injury incurred.

"And now, my Princess?" Biggy asked, helping her to her feet.

"I should like another mead," she said, nodding to the bar.

The men stayed naked and the Princess let it all hang out. After the act the atmosphere became more relaxed and the men spoke freely.

Princess White teased at the hair of Biggy as she lay against him, having found her true champion amidst a throng of potential mates.

As the mead and ale flowed the warmth in her core remained. It was a beautiful reminder of the act and when-ever she focused on the multiple loads inside her a sinful smile stretched across her lips.

She looked at the men about her and thought herself so lucky. They charged their glasses in her honor and took hearty swigs, making the Cock and Bucket their own until the owner's timely return.

What should tomorrow hold for the Princess? 'Twas anyone's guess.

THE END

GET ACCESS TO OVER 20 MORE FREE EROTICA DOWNLOADS AT SHAMELESS BOOK DEALS

Shameless Book Deals is a website that shamelessly brings you the very best erotica at the best prices from the best authors to your inbox every day. Sign up to our newsletter to get access to the daily deals and the Shameless Free Story Archive!

Jess needs more from her sex life.
Ever since she caught a glimpse of an orgy at a friend's party,
sex with her friend/lover Shawn isn't enough anymore.
Luckily for her, Shawn also has friends. Hot, horny friends,
more than willing to lend her a hand and more, and open the
doors to a larger sexual world.
A world where sex is for more than two, and pleasure is a
group activity…

~

"**G**od, that was amazing!" Shawn said, still trying to catch his breath as Jess climbed off of him and rolled over to the other side of the bed.

"Yeah…" She'd barely heard him, still high from her sequence of climaxes, the images of her fantasy still burning in her mind. He was speaking, his voice slurring and dragging, obviously still as drunk on pleasure as she was, but she didn't hear a word he was saying.

"Jess? Are you listening to me?" she finally managed to grasp him asking.

"Yeah, yeah... I'm here. Sorry, I was just... miles away," she said with a sigh.

He let out a laugh, more for emphasis than actual mirth.

"That's reassuring. My manhood is wounded, Jess. Thank you."

Her laugh, however, was genuine, and she sloppily slapped his shoulder.

"No, silly. You were great. This was great. You know it's always great, I just had this... thing I was thinking of."

His lips parted in a wide, knowing smile.

"Ah. I bet I know what. Still the Hayley thing, yeah?"

"Yeah... God, that was so hot..."

A week before, Jess had gone to a party with a few of her college friends, including her classmate Hayley. It was a normal party for that crowd. Rowdy, fun and occasionally sexy, but nothing too out there. Jess mostly stayed out of the sexy parts, choosing to secretly watch from afar whenever she could, her little secret thrill. That night, however, she had seen more than she expected. When she went upstairs to pick up her coat and leave, she passed the main room and heard the familiar noises of good sex coming from inside. And a particular moan sounded a lot like Hayley.

It wasn't that Jess had any yearning to watch Hayley have sex. But she felt the tension that came with her secret thrill, and she couldn't resist. She opened the door as silently as she could, just to take a quick peek. And her jaw dropped.

There were a lot of people in the room. Six or seven, she was too distracted to count. Their bodies were so mingled with each other she wasn't sure she could've counted anyway. Some boys, some girls, some that probably identified as neither, all fucking each other, regardless of gender or orientation. Everyone in that room was fucking or being fucked, and they were so wrapped up in each other that no one noticed the opened door.

And more or less at the center of it was Hayley. A number of hands ran all over her body, plus a few mouths and at least a couple of cocks, as she looked like she was in complete sensual overload.

None of it felt lewd, or dirty, or even aggressively sexual, somehow. In some way that Jess couldn't quite fathom, she instinctively knew it was all about love and sharing.

Jess had been turned on a lot before. But never had she been this turned on, this fast. She could feel her panties instantly getting wet as the image of the people in that room burned itself into her head.

She'd gotten home and called Shawn immediately. Luckily he was available, and by the time he had arrived, she'd made herself cum at least three times. She was still horny, he got horny too, and they had the best sex they'd ever had with each other. Then she told him the story.

A week later, she still hadn't told Hayley about it, since she knew her roommate liked to keep her sex life private, and consequently could react badly. But Jess couldn't get the image out of her head, as clear as it had been when she was watching through that door, and it was still as much of a turn on. And Shawn knew it.

"Yeah, I bet it was," he answered her, then paused before saying, "Have you ever thought of doing something like that?"

"What? No! I mean… no. Just… You know…"

"It's just a fantasy?"

"Well… Kinda."

He smiled.

"Define 'kinda.'"

She took a deep breath, trying to find the words that had already eluded her for a week. "It's just… Hayley looked so happy. All those people were there for her, pleasuring her, and she had completely surrendered to them, and she had this look of... I don't even know..."

"Bliss?" he asked.

That was it. That was the word. Hayley had looked in complete bliss. As good as Jess had felt during sex, or doing anything else, for that matter, she had never felt bliss. And she found that she wanted it.

"Yeah..."

He flopped onto his back and stared at the ceiling in silence. Jess did the same.

Had he taken this personally somehow? They were just friends with benefits, true, but he was still her friend, and she didn't want him to think he didn't pleasure her enough. Because he definitely did.

She was about to ask if everything was okay when he spoke.

"Want to try it?"

"What?"

He rolled over to talk to her.

"Really. I mean, we could talk to people we know, ask around. I can think of a few friends of ours who'd certainly like to get us in bed if they had the chance. We can let them, as long as they do it at the same time."

She laughed.

"No! Definitely not. I could do without sleeping with my friends, thank you very much."

"Oh?"

"Present company excepted, of course. But it's like, you do something that big with people you hang out with, and all of a sudden it kinda defines you. I don't want that."

"So you'd rather do it with strangers, then?"

"No. Maybe. I don't know..." She paused. Jess couldn't believe she was talking about this as an actual possibility.

"What if they're creeps? I mean, how could you even trust your own safety in a situation like that? No, I just couldn't." She looked at Shawn, and he was sporting a grin from ear to ear. "What?" she asked. He didn't answer. "No, what?"

"You trust me, Jess?"

"What kind of question is that? Of course, I trust you."

"No, but do you really trust me?"

She sighed and raised her hand.

"I do hereby solemnly swear, I fully trust you as both a lover and a friend. But come on, Shawn. You're a great lover, but you're not exactly a one-man gang-bang."

"True. But indulge me. If we were to do this, what would be the ideal situation? An all-out orgy like the one at the party?"

"No, no." She hadn't actually considered it, because she never truly believed she'd ever have the chance to do anything close to her fantasy. So the quickness of her answer surprised even her. "Maybe just me and three other people? Four, tops."

"Okay. I'm assuming I would be one of them, of course."

"You could be, sure."

"Okay. Any other girls?"

She had to think about that one. Jess didn't consider herself bisexual, but she'd come to that conclusion via experimentation, and as much as it wasn't her thing, she had to admit she had fun doing it. Still, somehow it didn't feel right for this.

"No. Just guys."

"Any type, or—?"

"God, I don't know! Hot guys! Gentle guys, kind guys. Guys who know how to treat a woman. Why are we still talking about this, Shawn?"

"Because I know people."

"I told you—"

He raised his hand to stop her talking, almost touching her lips, then he put on his softer, most reassuring tone of voice.

"No, no. You said you trust me. I know people I trust that could be perfect for this. Some old friends of mine. I don't see them that often myself, so most likely you would never see them again, no danger to your image there. Also, I'm pretty sure you'd be completely safe with them, but if I'm going to be there anyway, I'll make sure of that. I think I can make this happen for you, Jess. If you really want to."

She wanted to say no. It was something so outside her experience that she almost couldn't fathom going through with it.

But the thought that she would make her entire body tingle, and a familiar burning rise inside her. She wanted this. She needed this.

Jess moved her body closer to Shawn's, her head nestling in his chest.

"We're going to need a safe word."

"Sure," he asked. "Can you think of anything?"

She could. It was the only one that fit, really.

"Yes. Bliss."

FOR SOME REASON, Jess and Shawn hadn't really been together, either as friends or the other thing, since they decided to go ahead with the gang-bang, but they had talked every day, and he had kept her up to date with his progress regarding recruiting volunteers for the… thing, as she'd taken to call it. Apparently all the guys he'd asked had been eager to help. Who would've thought? At one point he had six volunteers, and Jess begged him to say no to two of them.

"Relax. They all want to do it, but this includes backups.

I'm sure one or two will quit for some reason in the meantime. If not, we can always tell them it's off at the last minute. They're prepared for the possibility, don't worry."

She was worried, but she wasn't about to let on.

As for her part of the arrangements, it had been easy enough. All she'd had to do was find someplace where they could do the thing. She found an apartment on Airbnb that was cheap, comfortable, available relatively soon, and also both close enough to the campus that they wouldn't need to lose too much time to get there, but far enough that no one she knew would be watching her. She set the date, booked the apartment, and told Shawn. Then all she had to do was wait.

In the end, Shawn was right. One of the guys wasn't available that day, so with much regret, he bowed out. Another was available, but it turned out that his girlfriend decided that open relationships weren't for her after all and what she really wanted was a more traditional boyfriend, to which it turned out he was amenable. So there would be five people there for the thing. Jess, Shawn, and three strangers that Shawn trusted.

He'd asked her if she wanted to meet them beforehand, for an informal drink or something similar. Something to make her more comfortable with them, and for them to get to know her. She considered it but decided against it. The whole point of going with strangers was to avoid any social pressure associated with the thing. If she became friends, or even acquaintances with them, there'd be social pressure all over again, at least in her mind. So no, strangers they would remain, until the day of the thing.

When the day finally came, Jess was abuzz with excitement and nervousness. She had decided to dress as casually as she could while still looking attractive. She'd also chosen not to wear any sexy lingerie. It would've been appropriate, sure, but for some reason it would make it less... normal. And she wanted to force some semblance of normalcy into it, something that she could hold onto when she got too nervous.

It didn't work, of course, nor did she really ever believe it would, but she was still glad to have given it a try.

The walk to the apartment felt way too long. She paced herself getting there, though not too much. The idea was to arrive on time, not before nor after.

Even that was making her nervous.

Then she got to the building, and saw Shawn waiting in front, all by himself. She couldn't help but smile.

"Hey, Mister," she said as she walked up to him, still smiling. He straightened at the sound of her voice, and returned the smile before he even saw her. "Whatcha doin'?" she asked, trying not to sound too forcibly playful.

"Hello, young lady." He lowered his voice, trying to sound older than he was, but ended up sounding like he'd smoked too many cigarettes. "Nothing. Just waiting for a friend."

"Just a friend?" She kissed him on the cheek.

He grabbed her ass, pulled her toward him, and French kissed her for a long time.

"A very good friend," he said after.

"Well. Someone's eager."

"Aren't you?"

Her nod felt a bit too quick even as she did it. "I am. Sure."

He smiled. "Jess, you don't have to do this. It's fine if you want to quit, really."

"I'm not quitting."

Shawn nodded. "Okay then. Let's do this."

He pushed open the door to the building and let her in. The elevator ride was silent, but mercifully quick. Jess found herself adjusting her skirt as she got out, then chastised herself mentally both for wanting to make a good first impression, and for thinking that it didn't matter because if all went well, because she'd be out of that skirt pretty quick anyway.

"Not too late, Jess," Shawn repeated as they neared the apartment door.

"Just open the door."

"Wait. Before we go in."

He searched for something in his pockets. What now? Her nerves were getting to her, and she needed to move on or she would lose her courage and end up quitting, which she knew she'd regret for the rest of her life. Yet Shawn was wasting time searching his pockets?

After what felt like forever but must have been only a moment, he pulled a black piece of cloth out of his inside pocket.

It was a blindfold.

Jess actually laughed out loud.

"What? I thought, maybe she wants to make it more interesting."

"Even more? No, Shawn. I'm going in with my eyes open."

He opened the door and showed her in.

"Then let's meet the rest of the gang, shall we?"

She entered and as planned, there were three men inside. Jess half expected them to be naked, but no, they were casually lounging in the living room, drinking and talking and laughing like what they were about to do was no big deal. Then again, maybe for them, it wasn't.

They went silent when Jess walked in. All of them got up at once, not hurriedly, just… politely. And smiled. Jess could feel their eyes all over her, but they smiled. She took it as a good sign.

"So, Jess, this is the gang." Shawn stepped between Jess and the men. "Gang, this is Jess." Then he moved towards the tallest of the three and put his hand on his shoulder. "This guy right here, he's—"

"Sorry," Jess interrupted. "Let me stop you right there, Shawn."

All four men looked puzzled.

"Guys… There's no easy way to say this. I don't want to be rude to anyone, but I'm pretty sure I'm going to. Still, I need to say this. I don't want to know your names."

"What?" asked the thinnest of the three men. "How come?"

Before Jess could find the words, the third man found them for her.

"This is meant to be about her. If we have names, we're individuals, and it becomes about us too."

She stared at the floor, too ashamed to look them in the eye. "I'm sorry, I know that's selfish, but—"

"No, no," said the tall guy. "That's okay. It's not selfish. It's how it should be."

"Yeah," said the thin one. "We're here because of you. You're the star here, not us. That's how it works."

She looked at them, surprised. All of them seemed to be in agreement. Even Shawn.

"Okay," she said finally. "Okay, that's… Thank you. Thank you for getting it."

"What about me?" asked Shawn. "You know me. How will that work?"

"It's okay," she said as she picked up a beer from the coffee table and took a swig from it. "I've had practice pretending you're not there."

They all laughed at her joke. She was finally starting to feel comfortable. Then she noticed Shawn didn't laugh with the others. He hadn't even smiled.

She put the beer down and went to him, then reached out and held his face between her hands.

"You know I was joking, right?"

"I know, Jess. Don't worry."

"You did all of this for me. I will always, always be grateful for that."

"Well..." Now he did smile. "What do I get as a thank you?"

She grinned, and he grinned back. He knew what she was going to do before she even moved. Her hands ran down his chest, unbuttoning his shirt as she went. She figured it was time to get started, and Shawn deserved to go first.

"Alright," said Tall Guy. "Let's get busy!"

Jess heard them move around, but didn't look, not yet. For the moment, her attention was focused on Shawn, her eyes on him as his shirt opened and her hands reached his belt buckle. They were still smiling at each other. Jess couldn't stop if she wanted to.

Her hand ran over the bulge that had grown in his pants. Then she opened the zipper, unbuckled his belt, and pulled out his cock.

Shawn's tip always got wet and slick with precum when he got really turned on. Which turned Jess on. This time, his tip was so wet there were strings of precum dangling from his tip to his underpants, which promptly broke as Jess grabbed the rod.

She had been worried that the non-familiarity of the situation would be a turn-off. So far, it wasn't, and Shawn's slick tip had the usual effect on her. She could already feel herself getting warm all over and wet down there.

She massaged his cock, getting him to close his eyes and moan. She was about to kneel and take him into her mouth when she noticed the other men.

Tall Guy had moved to her right, and Slender Guy to her left. Other Guy, the most normal-looking of the bunch, was almost behind her so she had to turn to see him.

They had all gotten naked. And, she immediately noticed, they all had their hands on their very hard cocks.

She could finally see them as the sexual beings she craved, and as she kept jerking Shawn off, she judged them as such. Tall Guy wasn't in the best of shapes, and if he had been shorter he would probably have a dad bod. But he was good looking, and despite being medium-sized, his dick seemed thick. Jess considered all she could do with it.

Slender Guy wasn't actually thin as he'd initially looked, but instead had a relatively toned body. He just had a slender shape. His dick, however, was the longest of the four men.

Finally, Other Guy. The one that didn't seem to have anything special about him. He still didn't. But he was good looking enough, and his dick was hard and apparently functional. He would do just fine.

Other Guy stepped closer slowly, until he was right behind her.

"May I?" he said.

Jess had no clue what he wanted to do, so she hesitated, even letting go of Shawn's cock. But they were all there for a reason, and the sooner she let go, the best it would be for everyone, especially Jess herself.

"Hm-hm."

She felt, more than saw, his hands reach for her skirt and undo the buttons at the side. The skirt fell to the floor. For one single moment, Jess felt exposed. Then she looked at the naked bodies and hard cocks all around her, which now included Shawn too because he'd gotten naked as soon as she'd let go of him, and remembered that they were exposed to her too. In fact, some of them were masturbating, which made them more exposed than her.

She liked that.

Then Tall Guy stepped up. He wasn't as gentle as Other Guy, and as he grabbed the hem of her blouse and pulled it up and off her, it wasn't as softly as she would've liked. But his cock was so hard it was shaking, and it looked very eager, so Jess guessed she could forgive him.

They'd naturally fallen into a circle around her. Four men gazing at her, all of them naked. Jess in her underwear at the center of the circle as they all touched themselves. All of Jess's fears and hesitations fell away at that moment. If it hadn't been clear before, it was now. Those cocks, those rock hard, primed for fucking cocks, were there for her. All hers, to do what she pleased. Or rather, to do whatever pleased her. Her body shivered with excitement. Yet for a moment, nobody moved. They were all waiting for her cue.

"Might as well get going, then," Jess thought, and got to her knees.

Not wanting to pick anyone over the others, she let herself move by instinct, and ended up grabbing Slender Guy's cock first. She rubbed it as he moaned. It felt good in her hand, but it felt even bigger than it looked.

Regardless, she put it in her mouth.

Slowly, Jess moved her head back and forth, sometimes dropping his cock and licking around it, just for variety's sake. She had always been an oral girl, and she could tell she was in for a treat. Every time she took him inside her mouth and pleasured him with her lips, she took him a bit farther in. Slender Guy put his hands around her head, following her movements but being careful to let her pace the blowjob herself.

As she blew Slender Guy, she sensed the others getting on their knees too. Six hands started touching her, massaging her, feeling her up. She almost couldn't tell who was doing what, and it didn't matter. What mattered was the feeling of it, the feeling of being touched and pleasured by all these men that somehow managed to find almost every one of her sensitive spots that wasn't between her legs, and it was amazing. Her whole body tingled, aching for more of everything.

Her eyes went up to Slender Guy's face. She could tell he was enjoying this. Then she pulled back, leaving little more than tip and the start of his shaft inside her mouth, and stopped moving. He looked at her, puzzled. Jess winked at him, and pretended she was going to bob her head again, yet didn't. He took the hint, and pushed himself in slightly.

"This what you want?" he asked.

"Hm-hm..."

He took over from her, moving her head along his shaft until it hit the bottom of her throat. She had no idea how much didn't actually fit inside, but from what she could see from her limited angle, it looked like a lot. Then he pulled out almost all the way, and did it again. He repeated the movement, each time going faster and faster until he was full-on fucking her mouth, somehow managing to never go too far inside, just enough to give her that feeling of almost choking that forced her to repress her gag reflex. Jess was pretty sure she drooled on his cock, but he didn't care, and neither did she.

As this happened, someone's hand finally reached between her legs. It wasn't Shawn's, she knew that much, because as the hand touched her wet pussy, she could feel that he was exploring while giving her pleasure, and it took a few moments for him to find her swollen, slick clit. Shawn always found it instantly. Still, whoever he was, he knew just what to do with it, as his fingers stimulated it perfectly.

The other hands kept moving across her body, and at least a couple of them were focused on her breasts, where she was very sensitive. They teased, squeezed, pulled lightly.

All this while her mouth got expertly fucked.

She had never dreamed it could be this good. And she knew they were barely getting started. Her mouth full with cock, she wanted but failed to moan, letting out only a guttural grunt.

Suddenly, she pulled herself away from Slender Guy's hands and moved back, letting his cock fall out of her mouth. None of them moved, all of them waiting for what she would do next.

"You," she said to Slender guy. "Get behind me." He smiled and did as he was told, positioning himself behind her as she got on all fours. "Who's next?" she asked. Before anyone could answer, Other Guy positioned himself in front of her. "Hi there," she said as she grabbed him and gave his glans a lick. His cock trembled, and she could see his body almost shivering. Clearly, he wasn't used to this either.

That only made her crave his cock more.

She wasted no time and took him in, while behind her she could feel Slender Guy's fingers caressing her wet pussy. She hadn't expected any finger play. What she'd wanted was that long rod entering her and going as deep as it could. But she had her mouth full, and it felt good anyway, so she let him have his way. As soon as his finger found her g-spot, she knew she'd made the right choice. All it took were a couple of touches for her body to want to buck and jerk in delight. She'd cum pretty soon if he continued, and as much as she wanted to cum for these men, it wasn't time yet. She wanted to enjoy the crescendo for as long as she could before letting go. So reluctantly, she let Other Guy's cock fall out of her mouth.

"No," she said, turning her back to Slender Guy. "Don't do that."

"You don't like it?" he asked.

"Too much," she said between licks of Other Guy's cock. "Not yet."

He took the hint, and immediately teased her dripping cunt with the tip of his cock. "That's more like it," she thought as she went back to blowing Other Guy. Unlike Slender Guy, this one didn't grab the back of her head, content to let her suck him off at her own pace. Jess had zero problems with that.

Then it happened. Slender Guy entered her. Even just a fraction of his prick felt amazing. He was going slowly, probably conscious of his length, but Jess pushed herself back, taking him further in. He took the hint and slowly went deeper, starting to thrust a bit harder. He was picking up a good fucking rhythm, and Jess found herself keeping that same pace as she blew Other Guy. For every thrust, Slender's long cock went in a tiny bit deeper. Jess's cunt felt incredibly full, yet she still craved more.

Somewhere in the back of her brain, she realized this was the first time she'd been with two people at once. It had always been something she'd wanted to try, but she'd never had the courage. Now, as she felt the waves of pleasure coming from both ends of her, it felt natural and complete. And as Slender Guy's shaft went as deep as it had ever gone, as she thought anyone could ever go, she felt the first pressure of a building orgasm growing within her. She wanted to surrender. She wanted to give in. Yet she knew Shawn and Tall Guy were doing little more than staring and masturbating at that point, and she chose to delay the pleasure and save herself for a better moment. So she pulled herself away from Slender Guy, and let Other Guy go.

"This place have a bed?" she said as she wiped the corners of her mouth of saliva and precum.

"Here," came Shawn's voice. Her head followed the sound, and found him pointing at an open door. She got up, finding it a bit harder than she expected. That made her worry. They were barely getting started, she'd only been with two men, after all, and she was already feeling tired? That wouldn't do. So she filed it away as her body wanting to surrender to pleasure instead of doing boring shit like getting up and walking, and tried not to think about it.

She strolled to the bedroom, trying to keep straight, without saying a word. She passed every one of the men without looking any of them in the eye. They diligently followed her in.

The bed was huge. Jess hadn't thought to check it when she'd made the arrangements, but it looked like they'd lucked out. It would do perfectly.

She yanked out the covers and flopped onto the bed. As she rolled to get on her back, the men arranged themselves around the bed, once again waiting for her cue. She smiled. These four men, these four attractive, horny, and extremely hard men, were all under her command. She loved that more than she could ever have imagined.

"Let's switch it up," she said. She reached for Other Guy, taking his hand and guiding him until he was in front of her. She spread her legs, surprised there was no hint of self-consciousness or shame in her anymore. "Are you hungry?"

"You bet," he said smiling. She pointed at her pussy and said, "Then help yourself." Diligently, he obeyed and proceeded to lick her. Jess's back arched instantly, every lap of his tongue a delight. She tried to get her own body under control, and pointing at Tall Guy, she called him over. "I'm very hungry too."

As soon as she grabbed his cock, she knew she would never be able to deep throat him. He was thick, thicker than anybody she'd ever been with. She wondered if he'd make her feel stretched out when he fucked her, and instantly wanted to try. But Other Guy was doing wonders with his tongue, so she decided to try her best to blow him anyway. He entered her mouth. It wasn't a comfortable fit at all. It was one thing to have his dick in her mouth, but if she moved to blow him properly she wouldn't just choke, she'd dislocate her jaw. So she took him out and licked his dick while she gave him a hand job. Not the same, but it would do.

Then she happened to glance to her side, and saw Shawn and Slender Guy there. Both had their hands on their cocks, of course, watching and presumably enjoying the show. Jess decided they'd waited long enough. It was time for everyone to party with her. To enjoy her. To tribute her.

She called them over. "You like my tits?" she asked Slender Guy, her voice trembling from Other Guy's licking. He nodded. She let go of Tall Guy for a moment, and gave her breasts a squeeze in his direction. "They're waiting." He instantly took over, massaging and licking her tits, a second tongue now giving her pleasure. She grabbed and licked Tall Guy's cock again, but with the other hand, she grabbed Shawn's for the first time.

Their eyes met, and she broke into a devious smile.

"I thought you only wanted me to watch."

"Never," she said, still jerking off Other Guy. "You're a part of this."

And with those words, she took his cock in her mouth, sucking him hard. He moaned loudly, drowning out all the other sounds of pleasure.

Jess realized then, she was doing it. She was really, truly doing it. Tall Guy in her hand, Shawn in her mouth, Slender Guy on her tits, and Other Guy on her pussy. She was getting serviced by four people. She was in a gang-bang all her own, and enjoying every fucking amazing second of it.

The thought alone seemed to send additional shivers across her body, but those were soon forgotten when Other Guy changed tactics, shifting his talented tongue to Jess's asshole.

"Oh, my God!" she let out. Nobody had done that to her before. It surprised her how sensitive her ass was. She'd had anal before, sure, but it was one thing to get fucked there, and another having a tongue eating her hole. She had no words to describe the feeling. But she definitely knew what to say.

"Don't... Don't stop. Don't stop doing that. Oh, God, that's so good." Then she looked to Shawn. "Do the clit." His hand immediately went to the right place, and he touched her like he knew she liked to be touched, while she alternated sucking him and licking Tall Guy.

Something clicked inside her then, as the multiple waves of pleasure crashed within her. She couldn't hold back anymore, and an exploding orgasm made her body buck and shake, to the point where she almost hit Other Guy's nose.

They all noticed it, she could tell by their smiles. A couple of them egged it on, even.

But none of them stopped pleasuring her. Which was good. Because as amazing as that orgasm had been, it had also been way too quick. Jess was far from done.

"Stop... Stop it, all of you," she said, barely catching her breath. She took her hand to her pussy while they waited for instructions.

"I need fucking," she said as she licked her fingers and tasted herself. "I need a cock inside me, right fucking now."

Shawn started towards her legs, but she grabbed his hand and kept him in place. He was confused, but didn't question her.

"Not you," she said. Then she pointed at Tall Guy. "Him. I want him to fuck me."

"Your wish is my command," Tall Guy said as he assumed the position.

He entered her slowly and gently. She was glad for it. As slick with her own juices as she was, he was a lot thicker than anyone she'd ever had. Long was one thing, long could hold back, as Slender Guy had. But thick was thick from the start, and needed more care. Thankfully, he seemed to be up to the job. He pushed himself inside her gradually, filling her in a completely different way than anything she had experienced before. She felt herself stretch a lot, but it wasn't painful, not really, it was just different. And very, very good.

Her eyes rolled with pleasure, and she caught a glimpse of the other people in the room. It was all it took to realize they wanted more. Just looking wasn't enough. Which was more than fair, she wanted them too, but at that moment the priority was letting her body adjust to Tall Guy's size.

Despite his girth, he wasn't very long, and soon he was all the way inside her. Neither of them moved for a while, waiting for her to feel comfortable. Finally, she felt like she had adjusted enough, and gave a slight thrust with her pelvis in his direction. He took the hint, and then took over, starting the movements back and forth, careful not to hurt her.

Jess moaned loudly. This was amazing. And as Tall Guy started fucking her faster, she threw herself back on the bed, stretching her whole body like he was stretching her pussy. It was time to call in the rest of the gang.

"Do me, guys."

Once again, Shawn moved to the head of the pack, positioning himself just above Jess's head, close enough that she could blow him upside down without ever needing to lift her head. This time she didn't push him back, and gladly tasted his throbbing cock.

The other two men decided to simply touch and massage the rest of Jess's body. It felt both exciting and relaxing. Other Guy was particularly good with his hands, causing tiny shocks of pleasure in places she'd never thought would react to that sort of stimuli.

Tall Guy was still fucking her, getting faster as she got more comfortable, and his thrusts made her head move and helped her blow Shawn. She could tell he was enjoying it, because pretty soon she felt his cock swell familiarly. He'd cum soon enough if she kept going. So she took his cock out of her mouth.

"Not yet," she said. Even upside down she could tell he had a puzzled look on his face. It looked silly from that angle, and she laughed. And somehow, for some weird reason, the laughter triggered her nerve endings, and along with Tall Guy's fucking and the touching of the other two men, it sent her to the edge all over again. She let herself go over that edge, and came so hard she thought she would break Tall Guy's dick off.

Perhaps because of that, he pulled back and out of her. She instantly felt the emptiness inside. That wouldn't do. Not at all. She craved to be filled.

Jess didn't say anything then. She wasn't even sure she could talk. She certainly couldn't control her body properly anymore. When she tried to reach out for Slender Guy, she ended up pulling at him so hard he fell backward onto the bed. No matter. It wasn't what she'd intended, but it would do just fine.

Somehow, despite her complete lack of coordination, she managed to climb on top of Slender Guy, and slowly get his dick inside of her. He went in easily, and she had to be careful not to let him get too deep too soon. Still, with her hands on his chest to keep herself upright, she started fucking him. He grabbed her by the waist and took over from her. She was thankful for that. Her body probably wouldn't respond to her commands to fuck him for much longer.

Jess closed her eyes and let herself enjoy the feeling. Then, surprisingly, she felt something else. Someone was touching her anus.

She glanced over her shoulder. It was Other Guy. His

finger caressed and teased her butt hole as he smiled deviously at her.

"Shall I?"

Jess smiled back, and nodded. His finger pushed slightly, making her ass open and give way. He pushed it inside easily. She'd never been one of those women with trouble giving access to her ass, and she knew that would serve them all well now.

"Not the finger," she managed to let out. He pulled it out immediately, and as Slender Guy kept fucking her, she heard a plastic tube being squeezed, and soon felt a gel-like substance getting spread on and in her asshole. The man definitely knew what he was doing.

"Hold on a second," he said. Jess was confused, until she realized he wasn't talking to her. Still grabbing her tight by the waist, Slender Guy stopped fucking her. As soon as he did, Other Guy approached from behind, and pushed the tip of his cock into her asshole.

"Oooooh," she screamed in delight as Other Guy pushed himself slowly up her ass until he was completely inside. Yeah, he knew what he was doing. Other Guy was definitely an ass man.

Mere moments after he was completely inside her ass, the two men started fucking her at the same time. They weren't in sync, but holding her in place somehow made it possible for them to thrust themselves into her simultaneously. Jess moaned loudly, her noises undulating in the air as she got fucked by the two men. She opened her eyes to see Tall Guy moving close to her, and at that moment she would've given anything to be able to suck him off, but settled for licking his cock and jerking him off.

Three men. Three men were pleasuring and being pleasured by her. It was glorious.

Her eyes searched the room for Shawn. He was the only

one left. She found him at the end of the bed, watching, still hard but not touching himself.

She winked at him. He winked back, and moved closer to fondle her tits.

As soon as he did, her whole body felt on fire, pleasure making every inch of her feel alive. She was cumming, hard. It was like she was cumming with every inch of her body at once, and it felt like it would never ever stop.

There was no rational thought left in her anymore. Her brain had simply ceased to function. She was nothing but a vehicle for pleasure, both for others and, more importantly, for herself.

It was amazing. It was the best orgasm of her life. And somehow, it kept going.

She took her hands off Slender Guy's chest, almost falling on top of him. But she reached for Shawn in time. He held her, like she had intended, as the other men fucked her. She felt a desperate need to kiss him, but it was physically impossible at that moment. It would have to wait.

Her body was still trembling. The orgasm itself had subsided, but it was like she now had smaller, instantaneous orgasms with every touch. And she was getting touched a lot.

Shawn moved closer, and whispered in her ear.

"Remember your safe word," he said.

Oh, she remembered. She felt it, in every inch of her body, of her being. She couldn't forget their safe word if she tried.

But she definitely wasn't going to say it aloud.

"Oh, shit," said Other Guy all of a sudden. "I'm gonna cum, man. I'm gonna cum!"

"Do it," Jess said. "Cum inside my ass. Do it!"

His cock moved and trembled in her butt, and she could feel the sticky spurts inside her.

He pulled back, spent, and let himself slip down and sit on the floor.

Maybe it was because he had the freedom to do so now that he was the only one inside her, maybe it was just the excitement, but suddenly Slender Guy sped up his fucking. Jess's mini orgasms had started to go, but that gave her a couple more. Soon, he grunted, and saying nothing, he came inside her pussy. For a second, she felt a hint of fear. What if this guy, this stranger, this tool for her pleasure, got her pregnant? But it was a fleeting thought and she let it fade away.

His cock immediately went limp and slipped out of her, but he stayed in place. Maybe he was waiting for her to finish. Except she wasn't the one that needed finishing.

"Your… Your turn." She forced the words out of her lips as she jerked off Tall Guy. He must have been close already, because a couple of tugs were all it took to make him come. He moaned and grunted loudly as white jets spurted out of his thick cock, landing all over Jess's torso. She couldn't judge properly because she hadn't seen the others, but she would've sworn he had the biggest load of the three.

Unlike the others, he didn't look tired or spent.

"That was awesome," he said, and walked away from the room. "There's still beer, right?"

He talked like it was over. But it wasn't. There was one man left. The most important one.

Getting off of Slender Guy, Jess moved closer to Shawn, and once again took him in her mouth. She wanted to fuck him, but both her holes had been filled by other men, and it didn't feel right somehow. So a blow job would have to do.

He just let her. He let her do anything she wanted. Anything she needed, with no complaints. And what she needed right then was him.

Shawn didn't last. Jess had long since learned how to

blow him just right, and he soon came in her mouth. She gladly took his load and swallowed it. It was less than usual. Maybe he'd cum while touching himself before, and she hadn't noticed? No matter. He came for her. That was enough.

Without saying much of anything, both Slender Guy and Other Guy got up and left the room, and soon were chatting it up and laughing along with Tall Guy. Probably drinking, too.

Jess felt completely spent. She let herself fall back on the bed, and laid on her side. With a smile, she took Shawn's hand.

"Come here," she said. "Get behind me."

If she had told that to one of the others, he probably would have fucked her again. But Shawn knew her, and did exactly what she needed. He got on the bed and spooned with her, his arms wrapping around her to pull her close. She cooed.

"Was it everything you wanted?" he whispered in her ear.

"Hm-hm. Thank you, Shawn. Thank you for giving me this."

"My pleasure," he said. She almost answered that no, it was most definitely hers, but thought better of it.

"Shawn?" she said, after a moment of silence.

"Yes?"

"I think..."

"What?"

"I think I love you."

He laughed. Not the reaction she'd expected.

"Sure is a weird time to let me know."

She laughed too. "I guess."

He waited until they'd both stopped laughing to speak again.

"I love you too, Jess."

"Good." She pushed her body back, getting as close to him as she could. For a moment, she wondered if she wanted to do it again, a repeat of that afternoon. And no, she didn't. Once had been amazing, but it had been enough. Yet her mind raced with all the other things she wanted to try.

As they both let themselves drift off to sleep, she knew that whatever she wanted to try, Shawn would be with her every step of the way.

And knowing that was pure bliss.

THE END

GET ACCESS TO OVER 20 MORE FREE EROTICA DOWNLOADS AT SHAMELESS BOOK DEALS

Shameless Book Deals is a website that shamelessly brings you the very best erotica at the best prices from the best authors to your inbox every day. Sign up to our newsletter to get access to the daily deals and the Shameless Free Story Archive!

MAYBE THE FIRST, BUT NOT THE LAST BY ZOE MORRISON

Kathy wants her first gangbang to be a blast... and it is when four hot guys take her every which way but loose!

~

I am not what you would call a good girl. I quickly discovered that I liked sex after developing the kind of curvy body that made men want to have sex with me. I am by no means a perfect ten. I am more cute than hot, but I have an above-average bra size, thick lips that, I have been told, look pretty good wrapped around a hard cock, and a willingness to spread my legs.

Some people would call me easy. Others would call me a slut. I will not deny being either. Most of what they say about me is true, I've sucked my fair share of cocks, been fucked by more than my fair share of men, and even let a few of them splatter their hot cum all over my skin.

However, it had all been on a one on one basis. Some of those might have been one-night stands, some of them might have had girlfriends, but the number of people involved always stayed at just two. Yet I will admit for just about as long as I've been having sex (which wasn't long as I was only eighteen) I've played around with the fantasy of more than one guy taking me at the same time. I thought it would never be more than just a fantasy, I mean what kind of girl would do that sort of thing? What kind of slut would let men fuck her like that? Just thinking about it started turning my lace thong into a wet mess right then and there.

I THINK my first encounter with the concept of a gangbang came in the form of reading my dad's dirty magazines. The first time, I reacted with disgust, yet the next time I found myself home alone I took out the stash and started flipping through them. I wanted to be the girls in the centerfold. I wanted to be like the women I found in the stories in the back. Women that had unforgettable sex, a lot more interesting than my own awkward and unsatisfying sex life at the time. The story that really stood out the most centered around a woman who went camping with her husband. The couple made a few friends and one thing led to another and five men fucked her and filled her with cum.

The next encounter came in the form of a porn video one of my immature guy friends put on at a party. From the woman's bleached blonde hair to her giant fake tits, everything about it fell into the category of fake. Definitely not a turn-on like the above story, but watching her take on four giant cocks somehow made the fantasy a little bit more real.

The most recent encounter with the theory of a gangbang came not too long after my graduation. Actually, right after. That night everyone gathered for parties, a wild night for sure but I do not think anyone had a wilder night than my friend Sammi. At one of the parties, she ended up sucking off half a dozen guys and fucking four of them. When I heard the story I reacted with disgust, but inside I wished it had been me.

However, I didn't want the whole town knowing I let a group of men bang me. Being easy or a slut is something you can write off as being young. Getting gangbanged follows you around. You'll go to the grocery store and someone will recognize you as that chick that let four men fuck you.

Yet, I couldn't stop thinking about the fantasy. It was the fantasy I thought about late at night when I found myself all alone in my room and no guy to call over. A fun fantasy, but nothing that I would ever turn into a reality. Or so I thought.

"I THOUGHT you said it would just be a girls' weekend," I said when Meg put down her phone. After a messy breakup, I was not in the mood to deal with any member of the male species.

"I know, but I didn't think Ted would be in town." She looked at me, then took a sip of her vodka and cranberry. We were house-sitting at her aunt's beach condo and had already put a major dent in her liquor cabinet. I wasn't completely sure how she planned to hide that, but she didn't seem to be too concerned. "What do you want me to do? Tell him he can't come over? That'll go well. I'm sorry."

"I'm sorry I'm in such a crabby mood," I replied.

"They'll just be here for a little while, then they're going out on the town."

"Who's they?" While I debated serious thoughts about never dating again, Ted did have some attractive friends - older, more mature, hot college guys. Maybe I could hold off on the dating vow of silence just a little longer; at least until I saw what Ted had to offer.

"I'm not sure. He just said 'we' while we were on the phone. He didn't mention who that included."

I hoped it included Alan. While he wasn't the college quarterback, he looked like he could have been, with a well-built body and guy-next-door natural good looks. The last time I had seen Alan it didn't go as far as I wanted it to, but we had done some serious flirting among us. Maybe this time I could seal the deal. With renewed interest in the weekend to come, I asked Meg, "How soon are they going to be here?"

"He didn't say," came the answer back.

"Damn you," I said with a smile as the funk surrounding me started to lighten up.

I RAN to my bedroom for the weekend and dug through my bag. We spent most of the day on the beach and after a cooling shower I put on a pair of old jean shorts and a well-worn tank top. Not exactly the kind of clothes I considered part of my dress to impress collection. I didn't pack much; I made the mistake of packing more bikinis than actual clothes. Digging through my bag frantically, I found a nicer tank top, a pair of linen shorts with fewer wrinkles in them, and clean underwear. Just in case.

I RACED THROUGH MY HAIR, makeup, and just as I pulled on the shorts the doorbell rang.

As Meg opened the door, I peeked out of my room. Ted came in with a case of beer and a kiss for Meg. Alan appeared next and I stepped into the hallway with a smile. He looked like exactly what I needed to get over my controlling yet cheating ex-boyfriend. Then three more guys came in, all new to me. It made me start wondering exactly who my doctor (Meg) had prescribed for me.

Ted introduced them as Stitch, Noah, and Ben. Stitch looked like the bad boy that my mom would hate, complete with the tattoos and jet-black hair. Noah looked more like a guy I could see myself dating and Ben had a fair-headed sweetness about him that, even though was attractive, not the nicety that I usually went for. I narrowed my choices down to Alan and Stitch.

The original plan had them just sticking around for a few drinks before heading downtown to one of the bars. At first, I didn't really mind that plan, however, after a few drinks with them, I changed my mind. They quickly reminded me why I was currently pissed off at the male members of my species. They hit on me and stared at my tits to the point it became uncomfortable. I'll admit at first, I liked the attention. It felt good to be reminded they were other men out there, but it quickly became more than I wanted to deal with that weekend. I was glad Meg was out on the balcony with me and that they would be leaving soon.

"I'll be right back. I gotta use the bathroom. Do you want me to bring you anything back?" Meg said as she slid open the sliding glass door.

"Another drink?" I had been pacing myself, but they made me want to drink more.

"You got it."

I thought she would be back after a few minutes. How long could a stop in the bathroom and a refill in the kitchen take? I didn't have a watch on, but it seemed like way longer than it should've taken. After Stitch undressed me with his eyes for the third time in a minute, I decided to take matters into my own hands as far as my drink.

As I opened the sliding glass door it was then that I realized Ted had also gone missing from the balcony. I feared the worst and my fears were confirmed when I spotted Meg's white bedroom door closed.

I didn't know what to do besides get another drink. I didn't exactly want to go back out on the porch with them, but the condo didn't leave anywhere else to hide. Before I could make a decision the four of them joined me in the kitchen.

~

THEY INVOLVED me in a conversation about beaches, but I barely took part in the conversation other than to nod my head yes. My brain told me they were all attractive, but they were acting like assholes. I knew they all wanted me, and I would be lying if I said I didn't want each of them physically. Good for a screw but not much else in my current state of mind.

I felt my body temperature rising and I couldn't be quite sure if it was because of the four hot men in front of me or the air conditioning couldn't keep up. I pictured being in bed with Alan. Sex with him would be a satisfying workout. Stitch would want to do something kinky, pushing me beyond what I felt comfortable doing. Noah would go out of his way to make sure that he satisfied me before he came and Ben, well, I felt that I would have to do most of the work with Ben because he didn't look like he had much experience, if any.

All four of them had selling points, but I couldn't exactly just grab one of them by the arm and drag him into the bedroom. Okay maybe I could, but it would be pretty awkward for the other three.

~

My next thought I wish I could blame on the alcohol; however, I barely had a warm buzz. I imagined myself on my bed with the four of them spread out around me - all of them naked and all of them rock hard and ready for me. The thought left my cotton panties damp.

As they talked about fishing, I completely stopped listening. What would it really be like to have all four of them? Would I enjoy it, or would they just use me? Thinking of them using me made me squirm against the counter. I took a long sip of my rose-colored mixed drink and hoped none of them noticed my excitement.

How would I do it? Would I just tell them I was horny and wanted to get fucked? The excitement in my body grew and my heart started to pound. How would they react? What if I just invited them to follow me into the bedroom? Or I could just drop to my knees right there on the kitchen tile and take one of them in my mouth to get the party started?

I probably could've dropped to my knees; Meg had completely abandoned me. Next time the two of us were alone, I planned to mention a few things to her. However, I didn't know how long they would be. They hadn't seen each other for a few weeks and probably had to make up for the lost time. Part of the reason that I didn't want Ted to come over was because of their relationship. They were a happy couple that couldn't get enough of each other. Meg and I were just eighteen, but I could already see the two of them getting married.

~

I didn't have a problem finding guys to date, but after a month or two things always seemed to get boring or I found reasons to end the relationship. I wasn't exactly ready to settle down, but I knew there had to be more than just one-night stands and flings. However, as all four of them stood around me, I didn't want a relationship. I wanted to get fucked and not just by one of them.

What would Meg say if she came out and saw me bent over the couch and them lining up to fuck me? What would she say the next morning if she came out and discovered all of us missing and my bedroom door closed? I told her everything. She knew about my flings. She knew about my one-night stands. However, she didn't know about this fantasy.

I could feel the blood flooding through my veins. The room felt one thousand degrees. My panties clung to my wetness. All four of them looked at me. It could either stay as a fantasy or it could become a reality.

I TOOK a long sip of my drink, still barely buzzed. I took a deep breath. I leaned back against the counter and pushed out my chest. "Guys I'm so fucking horny."

The conversation stopped mid-sentence. The kitchen was so quiet you could have heard a pin drop as all four of them turned to look at me crazily and their mouths dropped.

"What do you want to do about it?" Stitch quickly recovered from the surprise and returned to his cocky self.

"I want to get fucked." I couldn't believe the words came out of my mouth.

"I'd be glad to help you with that." He stepped forward towards me.

I put my hand out to stop him. "By all four of you." I've said some slutty things, but nothing would ever top that.

The four of them looked at each other, then me. It didn't feel real. I walked between Stitch and Alan towards my bedroom. I remember my bare feet touching the tile, then the carpet as I moved into my room, but it felt like walking through clouds.

∾

THEY FOLLOWED me into my room, Alan the last to enter. I looked at him and he shut the door. For some reason, I remember the decorations on the walls, all beach and nautical like seashells, and a compass that looked like it belonged on an old boat. I don't remember thinking anything for a few moments. Time stood still and they looked at me like hunters about to attack their prey. I felt like a piece of meat and I grinned.

They stepped forward and I stepped back. I fell on the bed. This was the bed where it would happen. Where my fantasy would become real.

∾

IT STARTED WITH HANDS. I felt a pair of hands on the buttons of my shorts. I felt another pair of hands grope me through my tank top. I looked up and saw Stitch between my legs and Noah's hands pulling up my tank top to reveal my orange bra. I wished I had thought to put on a matching bra and panties, but I don't think any of that mattered to them. All four of them looked down at me, their eyes filled with lust. A large bulge was already formed in Stitch's jeans and poor Ben, who I thought would be the least active, was quickly proving himself with a boner building not far behind Stitch's.

My shorts came off and my purple underwear followed. A new pair of hands joined in. I watched Alan put his hand between my legs, I felt his fingers brush across my pussy lips, and I let out a moan. I told myself to be quiet, I didn't want Meg to hear, but I knew that one way or another she would find out about this. He slid a finger into me and rubbed his thumb across my sensitive clit. My soft moan became loud. I bit my tongue as a last-ditch effort to silence myself.

A few moments later my tits were out of the cups of my bra. They hadn't even bothered to take off my tank top or bra all the way. Noah's mouth found one of my nipples as Ben found the other and I let out a cry as they both bit down and sent an electric shockwave straight to my clit. Neither of their hands was gentle and now their mouths weren't either. I usually hated it when guys went straight for my tits, but this time it turned me on.

When Noah released my nipple from my mouth, I raised my head slightly and saw Stitch again. He stood between my legs with his jeans and boxers around his thighs. He aimed his rock-hard cock at me.

I realized then that I hadn't brought any condoms. After the breakup, I didn't think I would be needing them for a while, so I didn't pack them. I wasn't on the pill and unprotected sex wasn't new to me, but this was four guys I barely knew. To get knocked up by any of them should have been a point of concern. I know that should've freaked me out, but it just turned me on more. I wanted to feel them inside of me without anything separating us. I wanted them to cum inside of me.

I OPENED my legs and watched as Stitch stepped forward. Time slowed down again. I felt his cock against me, and it felt like I could feel every cell of him against me. It made my whole body twist with excitement. He pushed into me and time returned to normal.

My wetness allowed him to easily push into me. He filled me and it was becoming real. No turning back now.

He grabbed my hips, and I wrapped my hands in the comforter as he began to thrust into me. I bit my lip, but I couldn't suppress the moans for long.

He fucked me for a minute or two, but before he came anywhere close to a climax he stepped back. Before I knew what was happening next, I felt another cock enter me. I looked up and saw Alan. Him alone would be a fantasy come true, but him with three other guys... this would be something that I would never forget! I'll admit there may have been one night where I had sex with my boyfriend at the time and sneaked out later that night to meet up with another guy. I always thought of that as one of the sluttiest things that I had ever done, but it didn't compare with what was going down now.

His thrusts became harder and both of us were starting to breathe harder and faster. Better than the workout I had imagined. He filled me with pleasure from the top of my head to the tips of my toes (and all in between!)

Right as I started to completely enjoy it, he stepped back, and I almost cried in frustration until I saw Ben was coming up next. All thoughts of Ben being sweet and less knowledgeable went out the window when he rammed into me like a cannon. He roughly tore into me and grabbed both my tits with both his hands. It was almost like I was a plow horse, and my tits were the reins. He was rocking me so hard it was getting more difficult to try and contain the sounds coming from me and my tits were getting quite a workout too as he pulled roughly on the teats every time, he barreled into me. It's always the quiet ones you have to watch the most. They'll fool you every time. I was getting into it so much that once again I wanted to scream when I finally felt him pull out and step away just as I was starting to again feel the pressure of release building inside but was abruptly halted. The four of them must have been talking about how to do this, but I don't remember any sound other than the hum of the air conditioner, the squeaking of the metal frame, and my moans.

～

STITCH, Alan, and Ben left me nothing to complain about in the size department, but Noah's erect cock stood noticeably larger. He pushed into me and I could feel myself stretching to accommodate him. I increased my grip on the comforter as he started to thrust into me. Because of his larger size, I almost felt that he was going to break me in two.

It was no longer a fantasy now and it was nowhere near over, but four men had fucked me basically at the same time. I had been gangbanged. I wasn't the run of the mill slut anymore.

I wanted more. When Noah pulled out, I flipped over and put myself on to my hands and knees. I didn't need to say anything else. Someone took me from behind, I didn't know who at first until I looked back and saw Stitch just as he slipped his dick into my ass. Noah came around to my front. He knelt on his knees and put his cock in line with my mouth.

I licked his swollen head, tasting a hint of his salty precum as well as my own pussy juices. I opened my mouth and took him between my lips. I then opened my mouth wider and took all of him into my mouth as Alan slipped underneath me so that he could place himself in my pussy. (I'm still not sure how he managed that with Noah at my head so I could suck his dick; I imagine Noah's balls were in his face.) Without realizing it, I then barely made out Ben inching his head in between Alan and me to lay his head on Alan's stomach so that his mouth was aligned with my tits and he began to maul them. The fireworks that were going off throughout my body were almost overwhelming. To have four men using me at the same time was bizarre. It didn't seem real. I felt one pair of hands on my waist another on my head. More than me sucking his cock, Noah was fucking my mouth. He used my mouth like pussy. They all used me for their pleasure, and I loved it.

AT SOME POINT, the pleasure of a cock inside of me, the feeling of a cock in my ass, and another sliding between my lips while a mouth alternately sucking, nibbling then biting my tits got to me and I lost it. The pleasure flooded my body. I closed my eyes and the climax erupted inside of me with a massive force that I had never felt before. I didn't know who I had in my mouth. I didn't know who was fucking me. Just feeling it sent me into a whole new world of pleasure.

MY OWN ORGASM was joined by another... and then another, and another and finally another. I felt two hard, almost out of control thrusts, and at almost the same time I felt Stitch shoot into my ass just a half-second behind Alan letting loose in my pussy. The force of my explosion and reaction to Stitch and Alan caused me to suck Noah like a vacuum which caused him to release next. He let go with such force that in my state on my knees with three other guys around me I couldn't drink it all like I wanted to so some hit me in the face and rolled down my cheeks but like a trooper, I did the best I could to catch all I could. Poor Ben, who was laying crossways on the bed with his head on Alan's stomach so he could reach my tits, came last because all he had touching his dong was his own hand and he was working it like he was trying to start a fire. It was sticking straight up in the air and when it went off some of it hit my arm that was nearest him. I heard a grunt and knew it was Stitch behind me. Seconds later I felt the cum splatter on to my back. The hot, thick cum hit me so hard that it almost made me jump. He covered my backside with his cum from near my shoulders to my ass. That asshole had masturbated himself again just that quickly and did it on my back! He then came around to the front and before he let me catch my breath he shoved his cock into my throat. He exploded again into my throat and somehow, I didn't gag once as his salty, cum flooded my mouth. When he pulled back, I swallowed it all.

I WASN'T DONE. I wanted Noah. I'd had him in my mouth, but I wanted his huge cock to fill me with his cum. I flipped over to my back and the other three already started to put their clothes back on. Noah however was naked from the waist down, his large cock still ready for me.

He pushed me into the middle of the bed and started to join me on it when I stopped him. I looked at Alan and Stitch and told them, "You've had your fun, but I don't think we have been very nice to Ben." Ben stopped and looked at me. I indicated for him to lie down flat on the bed. Once in position, I climbed on top of him and impaled myself anally on him then I motioned for Noah to take me from the front in my cunt. He climbed on the bed and the three of us were off and running while Alan and Stitch looked on. He didn't start slow this time. He slammed his cock into me with everything he had. It took a few moments for him and Ben to find their rhythm with one in my ass and the other in my pussy, but once they did, I couldn't hold back. They fucked me like I was their slut and I loved every minute of it.

~

I ENDED up riding Ben like it might be the last cock I ever got up my ass as I squeezed Noah with every muscle I had. My whole body bounced up and down between them on their cocks. I did everything I could, moving my body every way I could until he finally gave me what I wanted.

As a more powerful orgasm filled me, my body started to go stiff and I arched my back which made Ben underneath me thrust up one more good time and he unleashed his torrent of cum into my bowels as my body shook from my own orgasm.

~

HE ROLLED me off of him after he was done. I wasn't his girl-friend. I was some slut that he and his buddies had just fucked. They left me there, my whole body sore and exhausted, drenched with sweat and cum still clinging to me. I could still feel his cock throbbing inside of me when I heard the front door open, then close. I could still taste the cum in my mouth. They'd fucked me. They'd used me. And I loved it. I felt dirty, I felt like a slut, I felt alive.

~

A FEW MINUTES later I heard a soft knock on my door. "Kathy?" Meg asked.

"Yeah?"

"Can I come in?"

"Come in." I was already in my bathrobe, starting to clean up the room.

"Are you okay?" Her face looked concerned.

"Yeah." I couldn't hide my grin, I felt like I was glowing.

"What happened?"

"Do I really need to tell you?"

"And you're okay with it?"

"Yeah."

"You're such a slut."

We both giggled.

"I can't disagree with that."

"I never thought you would do something like that. How was it?"

"Words can't even describe it." I gave her the box score summary, her mouth dropped as I told her how it had gone down yet I think I saw some part of her that wanted to do it for herself.

THE END

GET ACCESS TO OVER 20 MORE FREE EROTICA DOWNLOADS AT SHAMELESS BOOK DEALS

Shameless Book Deals is a website that shamelessly brings you the very best erotica at the best prices from the best authors to your inbox every day. Sign up to our newsletter to get access to the daily deals and the Shameless Free Story Archive!

ORCHESTRATED BY STEPH
BROTHERS

22-year-old Hayley's decided that today's private lesson is when she'll finally seduce Mikhail, her cello teacher. When it turns out the lesson is anything but private, she fears her plans have been thwarted. However, in the presence of her fantasy man, and three highly respected international conductors, Hayley gets a chance to truly shine...and not just musically.

I laid in bed for just a while longer than I normally would on a Saturday. My cello lesson was in under two hours, and normally I was up and at 'em by now.

It had been nearly six years since Mikhail took me on at age sixteen as his prize student. I'd do anything for the man. His praise turned me into a goddess, every lesson.

But I'd finally decided that today was the day we'd forget about the *student* part. I'd simply be his prize.

The man was all hard-edged, intense Russian glory. He'd

been living in the states for longer than I'd been alive, but he still talked with his devastating accent.

He spoke perfect English, but it was always delivered with that steely, yet flowing, authoritarian tone.

I even loved how he mispronounced my name, even though it was just slight. Instead of saying Hayley, he pronounced it more like *highly*. I couldn't tell if that was his accent, or if he was making some kind of joke that only he understood.

Well, the only thing I knew for certain was that man was going to *worship* me highly by the end of my lesson. He'd never given me any hint that he wanted me in *that* way, but I was so hot for him, and his big hands, and his hard mouth. And I could be very persuasive.

Even thinking about him now got me slicking up a little. I toyed with the idea of rubbing one out quickly, but I needed to keep my hands rested for…well, for playing my cello, if nothing else.

I had my clothes picked out already. Low cut top, high cut skirt. And the cherry on top was that I'd be completely bare beneath them.

I couldn't wait to see his eyes bug when I parted my legs to glide my beautiful cello between them. Just the thought of breaking through that man's stony exterior got me soaking wet.

The whole drive over to his studio, I was squirming in my seat. For the first time ever, I was glad that I had to drive mom's car instead of mine. My little hatchback couldn't fit the cello in it.

The car was lame as hell, of course. But mom had one of those beaded seat covers, which normally I found ridiculous.

Today, though, *ridiculous* was not the word for it. A little bit of wriggling and jiggling, and those beads worked all kinds of magic on me. And even though it was city driving, I sang the praises of cruise control as well, for letting me free up my feet for a minute or two at a time.

When I pulled up at Mikhail's studio, I made sure to park with the rear of mom's SUV facing toward the building. That way, when I bent over to get my cello out, there was a good chance I'd…um…send Mikhail a signal.

Yeah, so I'm not really big on subtlety. But I had to use every trick I could think of to break through to this man. I wished I could say that I knew him well, and in a way I did.

Trouble was, the only thing I knew really well about him was that he was impossible to truly read. He was a granite citadel on a mountain top. So impressive to look at, and so hard to reach.

But there's no way he could resist me, today. I was a tightly wound string, and I needed his agile fingers to play the fuck out of me. Plenty of rough pizzicato. Not to mention long, slow bowing.

All my dreams crumbled like a landslide the moment I entered the studio, though. Mikhail was not alone. Far from it. He had three other men there with him. All of them around his age. All of them with that same elegant but severe charisma Mikhail used every lesson to devastate me.

They sat together, facing the small riser we used for concert rehearsals. I struggled for a moment with words and pressed my knees together for support.

"Um," I said, unsure what to make of it all. "Did we have, uh, something organized for today, Mikhail?"

He raised one eyebrow and brushed his long, elegant fingers back through his sexy salt-and-pepper hair. "Hayley, I would like you to meet my inner circle."

What the hell was he talking about? Was this some kind of cult?

"You should relax, sweet girl. We all studied together, over twenty years ago. These men are all conductors of esteemed orchestras. And we keep in touch when…there are reasons to do so."

He introduced the men one by one.

"Hayley, this is Anders. He joins us from the Norwegian Chamber Orchestra."

The first man stood, and bowed to me. He was slightly taller than Mikhail, but with a broader face, and a few more crinkles around the eyes. As if he spent more time smiling. Or maybe dealing with sunlight reflecting off snow.

"And this is Garth," Mikhail continued. "He comes to us from the Berlin Opera Company."

Garth stood and bowed, tossing in a little hand wave to go with it. He was maybe a couple of inches shorter than the other two men, and a little more solid in the body. But he was no less attractive.

"And finally, this is Noah. He is almost a local. He flew in from New York this morning."

Noah stood and smiled, looking a little more open than the other three men.

Every one of them towered over me. And they all had those delicious silver streaks coming through their hair.

"Hayley," Noah said, his voice a melodic baritone. "I've heard such wonderful things about your…talents."

"W–what's happening, Mikhail?"

"My girl, you have come so far with me. I would relish the chance to develop you further, but I fear I am being selfish. Keeping you here, all to myself, when you could go so far."

"I'm still not following."

Mikhail gestured toward the low stage. "Please, Hayley. Play for us. Let these men witness the beauty and magic that only I have seen so far. See if you can offer what it is *they* are looking for."

I swallowed my initial fear. Honestly, I was still buzzing between my legs from the seat cover on the drive here. And the anticipation of playing for Mikhail always made me as wet as a lake.

But the idea of playing for all four of these men just about had my arousal running down my inner thighs.

Mikhail opened my cello case as I sat on the chair, center stage. I made sure to keep my legs tightly together.

As my teacher tuned the instrument, I turned my attention to each of the other men.

Every one of them had a certain something that piqued my interest. They were very good looking, at least to me, with my classic daddy issues.

None of them was classically handsome, but they each exuded some kind of animal appeal.

I got the feeling from each man in turn that music was his coping mechanism. An outlet for passion. That when they weren't playing or conducting, all their desires and hungers built up inside them.

It was there in their eyes. As I flicked my gaze from one man to the next, I felt the heat radiating from them. Almost as if they'd stripped me bare of anything physical. That I was nothing but a soul on stage before them.

Mikhail stepped up beside my chair and placed the cello before me. He lightly touched my knee, his usual signal to spread my legs so he could glide that beautiful instrument between them.

Oh, god. I was already so wet, and that little train of thought only made me that much crazier.

There was no doubt in my mind that I wanted Mikhail. I'd happily stay here, year after year, and let him play me like I play my cello.

But I also truly wanted the adventures and experiences that these other men could offer.

And even though I'd come here prepared to bare all in an

effort to seduce my teacher, I was overcome with shyness with these other men here.

Rather than parting my thighs, I took the cello with my own hands and made sure it was strategically placed, before opening my legs and sliding it home.

Mikhail set up the music for Bach's Cello Suite No. 1 on my stand, and then took a seat. Normally, he'd be front and center, but this time he was a little off to my right. I guess he was giving the performance over to his friends.

It took me about a half a minute to settle my nerves and calm my breathing. I could do this. I knew it. But there were always nagging doubts.

I wasn't always able to play with professional detachment. Sometimes I lost myself in the music, reverting to a dream-like state. Usually when the vibrations of the cello caressed my inner thighs, and I pretended it was Mikhail using his mouth on me instead.

I bit into my lip to get my mind back on the job at hand. One more deep breath, and I began to play.

As happened every time I performed in Mikhail's presence, the cello somehow became him, in my mind. And as it purred to my touch, and sang between my widespread thighs, I couldn't help curling myself around it just a little. Drawing it closer to my body, holding my breath so I could press my breasts against the hardness of it.

I swayed with the music, closing my eyes and playing from memory, the long, legato passages gushing from my fingers, from my instrument, like hot oil.

Before I was ready, before I even realized it was upon me, I came to the end of the piece. I felt almost as spent as if I'd climaxed.

The sound of applause sliced through my daydream, and I pulled my eyes open. All four men sat, gazing at me, as they clapped my performance.

Mikhail let out a hearty bravo, and approached me. He crouched at my feet and caught my eye.

"I knew you could do it, sweet girl."

My entire body buzzed with excitement, the way it always did after playing well. The way *Mikhail* made it buzz, only even stronger than usual, with the extra men watching me.

He curled his long fingers around the neck of my cello and eased it out of my grip. I barely thought about what he was doing as he drew the instrument away from me.

The applause in the room gradually died away, and I came back properly from my dreamlike state.

When I glanced at my audience, I couldn't catch the men's eyes. Each of them wore an expression of rapture, of pure hunger. At first I swelled with pride, that my music, my talent, had captivated such brilliant and experienced men.

Until I realized they were all captivated by something else.

My naked pussy.

But rather than shame or embarrassment, I felt daring. Exposed, for sure, but empowered.

It was my playing that opened these men up. It was my body that enraptured them. And both were extensions of my soul.

Mikhail was the first to recover the power of speech. "My beautiful Hayley..." That was all he said, but there was a warmth in his voice that I couldn't remember hearing before. A legato as warm and smooth as the piece I just played.

He gazed longingly between my parted thighs, then closed his eyes and turned to face his colleagues. "Well, gentlemen. What do you all say?"

Noah was the first to stand. "Hayley, your playing is exquisite. *You*...are exquisite."

Anders and Garth leapt to their feet, as if their lives

depended on it. I made a quick scan of all four men and realized their cocks were giving me a standing ovation as well.

"Ja, ja," Garth said, barely below a shout. "You would absolutely be a most welcome addition to my orchestra, *fräuline* Hayley."

"Oh, Berlin?" Anders said with a scoff. "You will be lost in the crowds in such a landlocked city, Hayley. Surely you would much prefer Oslo."

"Hah!" Garth retorted. "And what, will she be going surfing in the waters there, Anders?"

Before the Norwegian could reply, Noah held up both his hands, as if making peace. "Come now, gentlemen. This is beneath us."

"You are right, Noah," said Mikhail.

"Besides, Hayley…you come with me to New York and you don't need to worry about passports, languages or—"

"Or any kind of class, or history, or culture!" Garth spat back.

Mikhail stepped between the men, and the infighting immediately stopped. Just as it was getting interesting. Dammit.

God, I'm a fucking hopeless case. I'd already started to picture them stripping off their shirts and wrestling each other, with me as the prize. And my pussy tingled with a fresh wave of arousal at the thought.

"Gentlemen," my teacher said, keeping his voice low but strong. "Remember who we are. And what we represent."

Mikhail's words seemed to quell the rising anger of competition between the men. He turned to me with a warm smile.

"My beautiful girl, after hearing you play, and…seeing you now, I find it very difficult to imagine letting you go. So, it seems that all four of us want you."

I rose from my chair and stepped off the stage. A few

more steps brought me right into the middle of them. A forest of tall, sexy men.

"And all four of you can have me." I unzipped the back of my tiny skirt and let it fall, baring myself to the attention of these gorgeous hunks. "Right here and now."

I instantly worked my tight top off and kicked my boat shoes from my feet. I stood there, completely naked, surrounded by four fully clothed, tall, broad-shouldered men. And I'd never felt more powerful.

The room was thick with silence, as though the air had turned to syrup. For all that these guys clearly enjoyed the look of my body, it seemed they were mesmerized by me.

So, I reached out and grasped Mikhail's rigid cock, through his pants. He grunted in surprise, but it eased to a deep groan of desire.

He'd been my teacher for so long, and he was the one who'd brought me to this place. Mentally and emotionally, as well as physically.

So it felt right I should give back to him, before the other men.

When I wrangled his zipper down, his breathing grew deeper and faster. And when I slid his flesh baton out, he cupped my cheek and sighed.

"Oh, Mikhail. You're so big."

"Hayley…"

It's true. He was really packing. But a quick glance at the bulges in the other men's pants told me he was about par for this particular course.

I was no virgin, but I wasn't the most experienced girl around, despite the attention I got from boys. Around here, the guys wanted cheerleaders, not music geeks.

I bent at the waist and took the tip of Mikhail's cock into my mouth, sucking lightly on it. The burst of masculine flavor sent shivers of delight down the length of my body.

I hauled his whole length deep inside me, until his rich musk filled my nose.

Noah reacted first out of the other three men, stripping all his clothes off. The others followed quickly, and then one of them—I couldn't tell who while I was so focused on Mikhail—grabbed my hips and squeezed them.

A moment later, hot breath coursed across the skin of my bare ass, before an even hotter tongue glided through the wet folds of my pussy.

The instant the deep, masculine growl sounded, I could tell it was Garth who had his mouth on me. He pulled my clit into his mouth and sucked on it like hell, and my knees trembled.

I stood, reluctantly letting Mikhail slide out of my mouth. He eased my disappointment by stripping off, letting me see the wonderful tone of his broad, strong body, and moan in pleasure about the wisps of silver in his dark chest hair.

Anders moved between us, taking my mouth in a deep kiss as Garth slid his strong, meaty hands up my body to grab my breasts.

Noah came in from the side and swept me up into his arms, stealing me away from the other two men. He kissed me, and I wrapped my legs around his body.

His hunger drove him on, until he slammed me back against the wall, the thick tip of his cock nudging right in against my cunt.

It was so tempting to just roll my hips, and let myself plunge down that glorious length of his. But Mikhail shouldered him aside, his face a mask of possessive determination, which only got me hotter than ever.

My teacher literally took me out of his friend's grip and placed my feet on the floor. He planted his mouth on the side of my neck and growled, as he slid his skillful fingers down my body, and through my soaking wet lips.

I was seriously struggling to stay on my feet, with all this wonderful male attention. As if sensing that weakness in me, Mikhail loosened his hold, and I drizzled to my knees.

With the solid wall behind me, the four men stepped in, forming a protective semicircle before me.

I worked purely on instinct, and curled each of my small, soft hands around a cock. Garth on the far left, and Noah on the far right. I stroked and rolled my wrists, and both men hummed with pleasure.

Then I plunged my mouth down the length of Anders's shaft, sucking and licking, coating him until he glistened like gold.

Mikhail fisted my hair and yanked me off his friend's length, turning my face toward his own shaft. And while I sucked on his cock, I kept my hands busy.

This was all so fucking perfect. Four magnificent older men, all to myself. My pussy was awash with arousal, and I couldn't wait for more. More of everything.

There was not a single hole of mine that would come away from this encounter untouched. I was certain of it. In fact, I relished the thought.

"Fuck, Hayley," Noah moaned, before dragging his cock out of my grip. He bent down and grabbed me again, lifting me like I was no heavier than sheet music.

He carried me across to the refreshment table, and Garth swept everything off the surface of it. Noah placed me on my back and stroked his gorgeous fingers down the center of my body, stopping when he had just one tip pressed to my clit.

"Ohhh…" I whimpered. "Please…"

I closed my eyes at that point. I wanted each man equally. It no longer mattered to me who was where, and which of them did what to me. As long as they all fucked me, I'd be happy.

With a mouth on each of my nipples, and another on my

pussy, I was in fucking ecstasy. But when the men worked together and dragged me lower, until my ass hung off the edge of the table, ecstasy became pure heaven.

One more mouth came into play. One of these devastating men flicked at my untouched ass with his tongue.

I lost the power of speech as they tortured me with their incredible skill. I could have sworn they were all flautists, the way they teased and tickled with their lips and teeth and tongues.

Their heavy breath filled my head with desires, and their heavier hands worked every part of my body they weren't already devouring.

They rolled me over onto my front, and let my feet drop back to the floor.

"Uhh…who's gonna fuck me, first, boys?"

One of them stepped up, and pressed the fat, rounded head of his cock into the glistening heat of my slit. And with one punching drive, he filled me like I'd never been filled before.

When his hips slammed into my ass, he let out a quick *holy fuck*, and I realized it was Noah.

I opened my mouth to moan with pleasure, only to have it filled instantly with the delicious bulk of another cock. Even when I opened my eyes I couldn't see which man it was. There was nothing to see but that big, beautiful cock.

He was kneeling on the table, pumping himself in and out of my mouth, and I took every fucking inch. All the while being driven toward ecstasy by the thick, meaty pole in my pussy.

Two long-fingered hands slid onto my breasts, one on either side. The way they squeezed and pinched was so different I had no doubt each one was from a different man.

God, I'd never felt so desired in my life. The fantasy of

truly having Mikhail's attention like this had always got my juices pumping.

In my naivety, I'd never imagined how it would be to have more than one man adoring me at a time. The reality was, it was so much better.

The big men wrangled me so easily. I was little more than a puppet of pleasure, and it was beyond perfection.

Behind me, Noah grunted and growled with effort. I couldn't prove it, but in my mind, he was a fellow string player. My bet would be double bass.

Those long, skillful strokes of his cock, so much like a bow biting into strings. None of the frivolous busy work of a violinist. He was all meat, all substance.

I was just about to reach my climax, and whimpered around the cock filling my mouth. Somehow, the men understood me, and they all backed off, leaving me suddenly empty, and feeling alone.

Anders stepped in and turned me on the spot, sitting my ass back down on the table as he guided his thick cock into my slit. He tightened his fist around my throat as he plunged himself inside me, his face a mask of pure pleasure.

He pushed me flat onto my back, still plowing away at my cunt. He worked his hips like a trombone slide, and he coaxed all kinds of sounds out of me.

Noah and Garth came in from the sides, biting and suckling on my nipples. I couldn't raise my head, could barely move any part of my body, but I desperately wanted to know where my teacher was.

"M–Mikhail?"

"I'm right here, my sweet girl."

"I…I want you to…"

God, why was it so hard to say?

"Tell me, Hayley."

"Please, Mikhail…fuck my ass?"

All four men dragged in long breaths and let them out with a moan. A choir of desire.

"I truly hoped you would say that, sweet girl."

Anders glided his incredible length out of me, while Noah and Garth stepped aside.

When I found my teacher, I saw he'd already taken out some lube, and coated his wonderful big cock with it.

I moaned with pure desire and rolled down off the table, standing on unsteady legs.

Mikhail took a seat and he beckoned me to him. I went straight over and turned around, straddling him. He steadied me as he guided his cock into place against my puckered hole.

"Gently, please?"

"Of course, sweet girl."

As I lowered myself onto my teacher's cock, Garth stepped between my thighs and ground his thumb against my clit, firing off bursts of pleasure that somehow made it easier for me to work Mikhail into my ass.

"You are such a beauty," Garth growled in his crisp German accent. "I need you now, Hayley."

"Then take me."

He lifted my legs and it opened me up, allowing me to take Mikhail's whole hot cock in my ass, in one long, liquid stroke.

Garth notched his cock into my slit and pistoned forward, and I just about screamed in bliss. The ecstasy of being so full, front and back, was something I'd never imagined.

Noah and Anders stepped in from the sides, and I devoured their cocks one at a time, relishing the flavor of my own juices as I drank from both of them.

Mikhail gripped my ass in his big hands, and spread me wide, bouncing me on his beautiful cock.

Garth gritted his teeth and hauled on my legs, pushing my knees up against my shoulders. I couldn't possibly be any more open to these men.

"Hayley, you are such a treat," he grunted. "Oh, fuck. I am…going to…"

"Wait…" I panicked for a moment, realizing how little I'd thought this through. "I'm not…and you're not…"

"Sweet girl," Mikhail said, his mouth pressed to my back. "You are perfection. And together, we will make the most beautiful and talented babies."

"Babies? But…"

"Would you rather we stopped?"

Oh, god. I never wanted to stop. Four big, older men, all worshipping my body like it was a shrine. All of them talented musicians.

Mikhail punched his hips upward, and I winced with the pleasurable pain. Yeah, it hurt, being stretched like that. But it was so fucking worth it.

"Oh, fuck…" I moaned. "Fill me. All of you. Please."

I gripped the cocks on either side of me and squeezed, as if they were handlebars on a bike. And as Mikhail drove himself deeper and deeper into my ass, I rolled my wrists and bounced my hips.

Garth arched his back and bellowed at the sky. A second later, he pumped waves of hot juice up inside my cunt, and I squeezed myself tight around him, to hold his seed inside.

And of course, every squeeze meant I tightened around Mikhail as well, and he hissed with what almost sounded like pain.

"Hayley…you are most incredible."

And, as always, his praise turned me into a goddess. "Please, Mikhail…fuck me harder?"

Garth moaned, and pulled out of me, dropping onto his

ass like he was totally spent. Anders stepped in to take his place, driving his cock back inside my cunt.

Every stroke of the big man's rod took me closer and closer to my own orgasm, but I knew I needed to hold that back. That was for Mikhail, and nobody else.

"You are beautiful, Hayley," Anders moaned, as he sped up his strokes. "You had me so close before. And now…uhhh…"

He gripped my hips and made long, fast thrusts, and my pussy begged me to let her climax. But I couldn't weaken yet.

Then the big Norwegian hammered his hips one last time, driving his long nail all the way up and jetting his oily fluid deep inside me.

No sooner did the Norwegian demigod pull out of me than Noah stepped in. He took only a few more strokes before he repeated the dose, pumping his wonderful cock in and out until he roared with release, filling me with another rich wad of cum.

He, too, fell onto his ass, with the other men.

Which left only my teacher.

Mikhail grasped my hips and squeezed like hell. He pumped in and out of my ass, faster and harder and deeper than I'd ever have imagined I could take him.

"Please, Mikhail…I want you from behind."

I slid up off him and dropped to my hands and knees, keeping my ass propped up so Mikhail could do anything and everything to me.

He landed behind me and drove himself back inside me. Only this time, he was in my pussy. As much as I'd love him to have cum inside my ass, his was the seed I wanted more than anyone's.

"Oh, my sweet Hayley…" he roared. "You are everything…"

There was no mistaking it. He was over the edge now, and going to cum.

"Please, Mikhail…fill me."

A moment later, he did exactly that. The sweet pain of being fucked so hard was everything I'd hoped it would be.

But the rich heat of his cum, firing deep inside me, just made the moment even hotter.

And that was all it took for me to plummet over the crest of my own wave, and dive headfirst into the most amazing climax I'd ever experienced.

I just about blacked out as the wave of pleasure washed through me, sparking every nerve, buzzing every muscle.

It was hard to tell how long I stayed there, on my hands and knees, my head resting on the floor and my pussy so fucking full of cum.

Finally, I lifted my head, and it was like waking up. Coming out of a bizarre but beautiful dream.

"Did that…really just happen?" I asked.

"Absolutely, sweet Hayley," said Mikhail, his voice dry and raspy.

"Thank fuck," I replied.

We all dressed, and I kept my legs pressed together. Holding in all that rich, fertile seed. Maybe it wouldn't take this time. But maybe it would.

"Have you decided what you want, Hayley?" Mikhail asked me. "Where you will go, or whether you will stay with me?"

"Not yet." I gave him a quick wink. "But I'm open to more…*discussion*. Is tomorrow good for you gentlemen?"

They all smiled, and Mikhail nodded.

"Tomorrow will be perfect."

THE END

GET ACCESS TO OVER 20 MORE FREE EROTICA DOWNLOADS AT SHAMELESS BOOK DEALS

Shameless Book Deals is a website that shamelessly brings you the very best erotica at the best prices from the best authors to your inbox every day. Sign up to our newsletter to get access to the daily deals and the Shameless Free Story Archive!

TAKEN! BY THE MOVERS BY ELIZA DEGAULLE

Grace gets the job offer of a lifetime and has to move across the country in a hurry. She hires the Bareback Movers, whose rates seem too good to be true. When she realizes she's going to come up a bit short after the work is done, the movers intend to get their moneys worth out of Grace, as recklessly, rough, and complete without protection - and leaving Grace with a night she's never going to forget.

"I got the job? I got the job!" I squealed and leaped a good five feet into the air at the moment, and then panickily rushed back and forth, overjoyed by anything and everything that was happening.

Of course, I couldn't bounce around my home too much, because there really wasn't a whole lot of home to begin with.

A tiny city apartment, but oh, this would be changing.

The offer done, the details coming in the email, I was ecstatic.

This had been a long time coming, the next step into my future as an adult, a woman. An actual career instead of a job.

It just so happened that it was across the country.

The only thing keeping me here was my parents, but they were so controlling of my life that I think a little distance between us would do all of us some serious good.

I clicked around my laptop and went for the next step of logistics.

Moving.

Across the country.

It was never as easy as it seemed.

It was expensive, daunting.

Thankfully, my employers seemed to have understood this and were promising me a nice big advance for my move. There was also the fact that I was a single woman with no particularly strong friends. I needed some big man arms to take care of all this. I guess big woman arms would be acceptable too, but my mind had all too often been drifting to the thought of jacked men sweeping me off my feet.

The thing I needed most now that my employment was taken care of was a date.

I figured that could wait, as crushing as the loneliness and yearning for a man could be though.

I flipped through the options. They were numerous but none of them were catching my attention.

Until I came upon the ad for them.

Bareback Movers.

The only protection your move needed was their steady and skilled hands.

Felt odd, but they certainly did seem cheaper than the other options that I could possibly choose.

Plus they advertised with hot guys. A literal cornucopia of beautiful men. They were all short-haired, yes, but I figured that was simply due to their job as movers. No one wants a lock of hair getting in their eyes when they are moving a dresser. Plus it gets all sweaty and troublesome... like the rest of them.

One of them was a damn Adonis of pure muscle, the other was a bit chubbier, but still looked strong as hell, a more down to earth superman. One was leaner, but still looked like he could carry the world on his shoulders, and even a black one looked like he could match the sheer power of all his peers. All of them just... majestic. Or scrumptious. Or some other word that just reiterated how wonderfully hot they were.

Focus, Grace, focus. Just because they're hot doesn't mean they should be hired.

More research. They had solid ratings unlike other budget movers. That was good.

The price, though. That was my rationalization. With that I could pocket the rest and use it as a safety blanket or potentially buy something nice for myself.

So I gave in. I clicked through. I ordered my weird, hot, cheap movers.

And I was thrilled at the aspect of meeting them.

As well as the new job, of course. Mainly that. At least that's what I kept telling myself.

THE DRIVE WAS LONG, the journey difficult, but I was finally there. My brand-new apartment.

Sure, it wasn't much bigger than my old one, but it was mine, and it was thousands of miles away from the repression of my very strict parents. I could finally cut loose and call it my own. Enjoy life how I wanted to enjoy it and all that.

I had found my seat watching the progression of movers

march past me. All of them were how they were pictured, all of them so enticing and delectable. I tried not to stare too much, not wanting to come off as creepy and too flirty.

But I don't think they carried the same restraint. "Pardon me, ma'am," the thicker of the men said to me. He accompanied his words with a grin and a sly cocking of his eyes.

"Oh sorry," I said, moving my legs out of the way.

"It's fine, a girl like yourself can't help if their thick thighs get in the way sometimes." The flimsy name tag on his sleeveless shirt said Chris.

He continued on past me, and I was left sitting there wondering what his words actually meant. Was that a flirt? A backhanded compliment? Not a compliment at all? All of it seemed so overwhelming and confusing to me.

It was hurting my head, so I got up and headed into the kitchen. As I walked, I felt the strangest sensation that I was being watched. I turned around and looked back. At Ty and Greg, the muscle-bound ones of the group, strolling by with another one of my dressers. They looked away as I did, and again, I was wondering if they were checking me out.

No. They couldn't have been. That was kind of absurd, honestly. All four of them could just shoot any woman on the planet a look, and instantly have them. And me? Simple average plain jane generic Grace? It didn't seem like something that they would actually entertain, honestly.

I mean, I wasn't even barely legal or anything. I was twenty. I didn't even have the allure of breaking the law on my side anymore. I would have to work hard to catch a guy's attention, and use things like, I don't know, my personality or something crazy like that. The thought of relying on such a thing instead of just being boring and hot didn't sit well with me.

I dug one of the few things already there, a diet soda, out of the fridge, and proceeded to drink it down, that eerie feeling of being watched still nagging at me randomly. This was one small job out of hundreds they've done. They couldn't have been thinking I was special or something for them, or anything like that?

The whole operation didn't take all that long really. I didn't have all that much stuff to move, and soon I was facing all four of them, their arms crossed and peering down at me.

"Your bed is set up now, by the way, Ms. Grace. Everything is good to go, and now we simply await for you to pay and send us on our way." Chris said, his grin, like seemingly all the others, oh so permanent.

"Thank you so much. You worked quickly." I wasn't in any rush to see them go or anything, but I guess my brief encounter with these hot guys was almost over. I dug into my wallet, fished out my card, and handed it over.

Chris handed it off to Ty who ran off to do whatever tech stuff needed to be done to process it. Leaving me with the bearing eyes of the other men in the room, looking down at me and ready to devour me whole.

"So," the Adonis-like one, Greg, said, "you're going to be living here alone, I presume?"

"Yeah. A little bit of solitude will be nice after years of having my parents so near. I figure I can always go look for a roommate if the loneliness became too much."

"A girl like you? Lonely?" Ryan, the leaner of them added. "Girl, you never have to be lonely. There's plenty of men all around who would be nuts about spending the night with you."

"Yeah, uh, well, um..." I smiled earnestly about it. There weren't too many ways to interpret that line and it was quite overwhelming about how he was coming at me. "Just um..."

"Should be beating them off with a stick or something," Chris added. "Like, all four of us haven't been able to keep our eyes off you this whole time."

And there it was. Confirmation about what I suspected. I was being watched. Lustfully and needfully.

In my travels to my job, did I cross over into the bizarro world? Where I went from a slightly overweight girl no one would bat an eye at to becoming some sort of super model?

I was pinching myself too, just in case it was the dream thing.

Finally, my bewilderment was broken up by Ty returning with my card. "Uh, Miss, I got some bad news for you. Your card was rejected."

I stared at him, wide eyes and unblinking. "What? What do you mean?"

"Insufficient funds. You don't have enough money in your account."

"You can't be serious."

"I am serious. I wouldn't joke with you, miss, I'll be completely honest, I quite enjoy getting paid. Not as much as I enjoy other things mind you, but getting paid is up there."

He gave it back to me, and I just stared at it.

How could I not have enough money on my card? That was absurd. Were they running some sort of scam?

I glanced up at all of them, them watching me inquisitively with smiles, waiting for what I was going to do next. They didn't seem anywhere near as annoyed that they might not have been being paid than they should have.

So I grabbed my phone. I went to my bank's app. I brought up my account.

Sure enough, the money wasn't there. A sense of dread was boiling inside of me.

"Pardon me, gentlemen, I'll be back in a moment."

In a rush, I dialed up my employers. I needed an answer, what was the hold up, what was causing all this trouble now?

"Hello? Frank? Can I talk to Frank?"

"You're talking to him."

"Frank, I thought you were paying me a signing bonus for taking this job?"

"Yes. We are."

"Then where is it? It's not in my bank account like it all said."

"One problem there, toots..."

Did... did he just call me toots?

"You don't get the bonus immediately, babe. What if you agreed, we gave it to you, and you quit immediately? We gotta be safe about it. No, you don't get the bonus until you work for us for a month, toots."

What the heck was with him calling me toots? "But I need that money to pay the movers. They're right here and waiting, I can't just sit here and wait. I need that money now."

"Sounds like that's a you problem and not a me problem, toots."

"You can't be serious, you can't do this to me, this is..."

The call ended.

"Not fair."

His words made sense, but how did they expect me to make this massive move without assistance? It was all absurd, but...

It was their right. Dammit.

I paced back and forth in the kitchen, trying to think of what the hell I was going to do about this. They were there and waiting for their money, and I couldn't come up with the total they were asking for. No way, no how.

As much as I wanted to panic to an absurd degree, I had to face the music. Maybe I could convince them to go onto a payment plan, or an IOU.

Maybe they'd pick up all my stuff and dump it out on the street out of spite.

Whatever it was, I couldn't run away forever. By delaying

it all I was wasting their time, as well as my own in any picking up of the pieces.

My feet were lead in plodding toward my death sentence.

"Uh," I said, my mouth hanging open as I trudged out into the living room area where they waited "Uh.. um..."

"Spit it out, dear, is there a problem?"

"So, um, I totally misjudged when I'd be getting the bonus for this job, and uh..."

The four of them shared a knowing glance with one another.

"You don't have the money?" Chris said, an eyebrow cocked.

I sank, my heart low. "No. No I don't."

"That's rough," he replied, rubbing his chin in disappointment.

"Is there an IOU system? Or maybe a payment plan? I'm really sorry. I didn't expect them to go and do this to me at all."

"That's really rough. We don't do any of those things. We're pretty in and out about this sort of thing. No one you can borrow money from? Like a parent or whatever?"

Ew. My parents might have been able to help out, but they'd probably like, demand daily video calls and whatever else for their cooperation.

And that was a maybe. We did leave off on a nasty fight, and it wasn't like my parents were ludicrously loaded.

"So I'm going to guess that's a no on the rich parents thing?" Chris said, stepping toward me, and towering over me. I felt meek and powerless before him as well as his three very hot, very strong friends.

"Uh...I'm really sorry. Just... let me pay you back somehow."

They shared another glance at one another, the smiles still on their faces.

Then, all of a sudden, they struck.

Chris pulled me toward him, his big strong arms literally sweeping me off the ground and taking me off my feet, his lips on mine, overwhelming me with his movements.

His kiss was so powerful, forcing my eyes wide, his tongue pushing in, urging mine to follow him and me so helpless but to do anything but give into him.

"If you can't pay us with your money, girl," Ty said, approaching me from behind. "You're going to pay us with your body."

"My - my body?" I stammered as I breathlessly broke away from the kiss.

What was going on? Ty was wrapping his arms around my waist from behind, his lips descending on me, and kissing my shocked face powerfully and intensely.

We immediately went from me being utterly unable to pay for any of this, to them suddenly kissing me. To make me pay with my body.

It all felt so sudden, it all felt so absurd.

"I was hoping it'd come to this," one of them said, my attention stolen away by the ravishing kisses coming from Chris and Ty.

The phrasing of their words, it was so odd. Was this something that they did regularly? Was it really a common problem for people to be unable to pay? My mind was awash with questions of logic, but that was quickly being pushed aside with thoughts of what this was leading to.

I was being carried toward my bed, and soon enough, I was bouncing off of it. Chris was still on top of me. "What's going on?" I managed to let out in the chaos of the moment.

"We told you," he said. "You can't pay us with money, so all four of us are going to get our proper use out of your body instead. We're going to enjoy you however we want you, Grace. We think it's a fair exchange for us not getting paid today, right boys?"

The rest of them cheered.

My adrenaline was pumping, wondering what I should do. This was clearly in some blurry area of consent where I should be screaming no and telling them to fuck off, and yet?

I didn't want to. Their proposition seemed to have been everything that I wanted, what I had been idly fantasizing about ever since I had seen their ad online.

He was pushing my shirt up my torso, and my arms were rising up above my head, my bra exposed to them, and they immediately started to tease and play with them as they were exposed. They were laughing as their fingers touched my body, and looked at what I had.

I hadn't chosen my clothing for any sort of special occasion. It was all pure comfort for an eternal ride across the country to what was supposed to be the start of something new and exciting.

I guess in a way, that's exactly what it was, but I definitely didn't expect it to all turn out like this.

It all happened so fast, one moment I'm in financial peril, then I have four men all over me quite literally saying they all planned to fuck me for their payday.

Each of their hunger for me is clear. Greg pulls off my bra, and takes a whiff of it, getting the tiniest tastes of my aroma, my scent. It seems to only intensify his need for me. Ryan helps Chris pull my legs up, stripping off my shoes, my socks, my jeans, all of it until I'm all of a sudden sitting in front of them in only panties, so very intimidated and wondering what is to come next.

All of them looked down at me. Licking their lips. Very obvious bulges in each of their own jeans, all of them ready to descend on me and indulge in me.

"If you haven't figured it out, Grace," Chris said, "We're

not in this for the money. We're all pretty well-off in our own way. We charge less to provoke situations like this. To offer alternative ways to pay, to enjoy women who need a bit of help with their move but lack the funds to make it happen."

"If they can pay, sure, we'll back off," Ty added. "We hope that's the case if they're a dude or if it seems like someone we wouldn't have a terrible amount of fun with. But girls like you, Grace?"

"You're our ideal customer, babe," Ryan said. "We did you a great favor, and it's only fair you repay us by spreading those legs of yours, and letting us fulfill our lusts with you."

"Bareback, raw," Greg finally chimed in. "We showed the most tender of care with your furniture, but you? Unlike a dresser, you'll heal. Unlike a dresser, you'll end up liking everything we do."

I swallowed a big gulp. Did I even have a say in this? I really couldn't pay them to go away, and I had to say the fire that was kindling inside me was all too intense.

They were offering me everything a young woman like myself could ever want.

So I happily obliged, unsure of if I had any real choice in the matter anyway. I spread my legs for them, and in near synchronization, they took off their shirts one by one.

All of their manliness, their chests, glistening calling out to me to indulge in them.

I didn't get the chance to gawk at them for long before Chris was right back on top of me, his powerful form, pressing against mine, and consuming me so. His hand going up my thighs, to my pussy.

He immediately set the tone to what he was out to do. His touch powerful and harsh, right down on my sex, his hand pushing into me, the friction of the moment so immense as he goes deeper and deeper down there. His fist balls up, grabbing the fabric of them and pulling them right down my leg, demanding my cooperation or that he would simply rip them right off me.

I was all too happy to help him along, for him to strip me of them in an instant, flinging them toward a nearby wall.

He hammered on me not caring, his fingers going right toward my clit, and rubbing me hard, rubbing me fast.

The fire that was inside me was building bit by bit, flooding through me, urging me higher and higher, pushing me up my orgasmic mountain quicker and quicker, everything growing more intense by the moment.

Chris's smile only grew as the intensity of the moment grew hotter and hotter inside me, whipping in and around me again and again as I struggled to keep myself together through it all.

The electricity inside me was roaring, rushing, and burning out of control through me. I wasn't the most experienced of girls in the realm of sexuality. I could count the amount of boyfriends I had on one hand and not all of them made it to even second base.

Chris, though, he would be no like no boyfriend I would ever have. Rough, only using my pleasure as his entertainment. Rubbing me harder, faster, inching me more and more, causing me to cry out in some sort of joy.

All focused on my clit, seemingly racing to see how fast he could make me cum.

God, was he doing it.

All too fast it rushed at me, it hit me. The intensity of it all caused me to cry out suddenly, briefly, wonderfully.

It surged through me, sending me high, before I floated back down, surrounded by them, laughing like all of this was just a grand ol' time.

"She comes pretty fast. She's going to be a lot of fun," Ty said, nodding, unzipping his jeans and the rest of them following suit. A sea of bulges underneath boxers, boxer-briefs, a set of tighty whities, and uh...

Well no bulge at all since one decided to go commando.

Ryan stroked his cock as he approached me. "I knew she was going to be one of our special cases. Just had the feeling."

"The chafing man, really," Chris replied.

"Don't bother me much. Just gotta keep thinking about what you're going to enjoy."

I tried to say something in response, but Ryan was swift to use his advanced getting-naked strategies to his advantage and was the first one on top of me. His hand sliding down my body, finding my clit, rubbing my already aching sex. The ripples of delight shaking through me again, he stole another kiss from me.

His tongue pressing in, forcefully demanding my attention, making me squirm beneath him as he pressed his body against my own. The kiss broke, only for him to make a loud declaration that was for his friends' benefit more than my own. "She's so fucking wet, guys. She's a freaking waterfall. She's loving every bit of this."

Every time I tried to say something to the contrary, I let out a moan. Them using my body against me so well, every bit of friction between us so potent and overwhelming. His chest against mine, the flesh tickling my breasts, anything and everything.

But they weren't here to make me pay with my body by just tickling me and seeing how fast they could finger me. It was pretty clear to me what they meant. All of them soon naked as I was, me lying spread eagle with one of them between my legs. His cock poking my slit, ready to impale me, ready to claim me.

I should have felt disrespected and used to be surrounded by all of them like this, being used as a glorified sex toy. Instead? I oddly felt desired. That all of them yearned for me to fuck up so that they could claim my body.

Then, in a sudden move, Ryan thrust himself in.

All of him.

I really was as wet as they said I was. Maybe it was the sudden fingering attack, maybe it was because this was awakening some unrealized fantasy within me, but I was absolutely loving what was happening right now.

All of him, thrusting in, all of him suddenly consuming me with so much blissful power. The electricity jolted through me then, making me scream out with delight.

Ryan wasn't gentle with his pace. He was immediately hammering into me with that cock of his, in all of its bare, naked glory.

My eyes went wide as I realized the other element to what was happening.

He wasn't using protection. There were no condoms in sight, and I wasn't exactly carrying my own supply to try to protest with.

Ryan was fucking me harder, faster. The intensity of the moment was just rising so quickly, causing me to scream in so much delight.

Harder, and I was right there with them, so sensitive to what was happening and the power of the moment. The fire inside me was growing stronger, ready to explode and consume me again, so soon after my poor clit was playfully abused.

He grunted as he fucked me, his grip on my hips tighter. Ever so briefly I wondered if he was going to properly pull out, if he was going to spare me the further risk.

No. No he wasn't. It didn't feel like that as he plunged himself deeper, and then proceeded to flick my clit one last time to send me soaring once again.

The fire rushing through me, the heights of the sensations all over.

Hearing him grunt so quietly beneath my screams, his grip went from tight to death around my hips.

And to feel his cock pulsate deep within me. To feel it fire everything it had, filling me to the brim, and then some. Every blast of that heat felt so damn sweet within me, the ecstasy I was feeling intense and strong.

The haze that came with what happened let me put off thinking about the reality of the situation just a little while longer.

That this might not be a simple spontaneous turn of events, that this might be far more than I really expected. Something with legitimate consequences that I might have to face.

And how sore I was going to be in the morning really didn't count.

"Fuck she's tight. A good fuck too," Ryan said. "Who wants my sloppy seconds?"

"All nice and lubed up for me? Don't mind if I do," Greg replied.

"Oh right, you're the weirdo who actually likes that sort of thing."

"Don't judge me because I'm well-endowed and like a little bit of the slippery love."

I stared up at them wide-eyed and amazed by all of it.

The big, muscly Greg was then on top of me. His size was encapsulating all of me. And I wasn't even talking about his junk. It was all happening so fast that I was barely able to really sit back and judge what each of them was coming at me with.

Just that it was more than enough for someone so inexperienced like I was.

"You're a little cutie," he whispered in my ear as he got close. "Been waiting for this since I first caught sight of you."

His cock rubbed against my poor, aching clit, it throbbed with his strength. Just like how his friend hardly waited for my approval, he slid himself down my sex before thrusting himself in.

It was a damn train bursting through me. A rush, his huge cock tearing through me and testing the very boundaries of what I could endure as a woman. All of my body was squeezing on him, passively trying to expel him with all his massive size.

But just fucking me like Ryan did wasn't enough for him, no. He had to take it further. He had to fold me up like a damn accordion. He was showing me how flexible I could be, bending my legs back toward my ears.

They weren't kidding when they said they were going to use me, that they were going to use my body as payment. It was all so reckless, so powerful, so abrupt.

I kinda hated that I was liking it so much.

Hard and fast, Greg took me, piledriving me with so much fury, every penetration sending a brutish surge of delight all the way through my form. My heart pounded faster and faster as the intensity of the situation only grew more and more fervent, and I struggled to cope with anything and everything that was happening to me.

Greg though just kept at it, every inch of my body shuddering from the impact of his cock slamming into me, the immense nature of it all, the intensity, everything.

Of course I couldn't resist him like this for much longer. Soon I was being pushed over the line, the intensity of it all coming at me so strongly. I let out a loud cry, mostly muffled by the bed beneath me, before I felt the sinful feeling again.

The tenseness of his muscles against my own. The flow between us, the rush into me, all of the heat, all of the seed, of its power just pouring into me. All of its danger, all of its uncertainty.

Then, like I was nothing more than a ragdoll, he pulled out of me, and let me slump down face first onto my bed. My entire body aching the good ache, every bit of the moment so incredible and intense. I nibbled on my lip, convulsing in joy of the moment, and how utterly ludicrous it was.

I didn't really get the time to savor it. Not one bit. The next set of hands grabbed my hips and forced me onto all fours. Those dark strong hands didn't even bother checking in on me. Slapping me on the ass, guiding his cock, which was just as big as the one before it, down over my back, across my sweat covered butt, and zeroing right in on my pussy.

They made it oh so clear what they all wanted. They were going to use and abuse me as nature intended. Maybe it was a competition for them, to see just who would manage to be the one who would knock me up after they all emptied their loads into me.

Ty was no different. Ty speared himself into me from behind, all of his cock following the path of his friends. Going deep into me. Parting my pussy lips and driving me a bit batty as I cried out with joy for what he was doing.

Very direct in fucking me, every thrust sending my body swaying, my breasts bouncing to and fro in a rhythmic motion. The rest of them watched me as I got so properly fucked by their friend, stroking themselves and enjoying the show. Even Greg and Ryan, who had already blown their most potent loads, didn't seem too set back from wasting themselves into me.

They were enraptured with me, riveted by me. This was all so sudden, but I was really these men's sexual goddess, all of them wanting a continued piece of me.

Harder, faster, Ty fucked me. Pushing the limits of what I

could take, making me question if it truly was possible for a man to fuck my cervix loose.

But that was an absurd worry. No, all there was to experience at this moment was the terrific fuckings I was continually receiving at their hands.

I screamed out in absolute bliss at that moment, crying out in absolute wonderful bliss. Arching back into Ty as he so recklessly pounded into me, almost slapping my ass in rhythm with every penetration. The impact of those shaking through my body, driving me a slight bit crazier and crazier by the moment, as my entire form was claimed for the fourth time by all of them.

My throat hurt from everything I had let out, how much I was pushed, but the orgasm kept coming. It kept coming at me seemingly long after my body should have given up and surrendered from all of it.

Perhaps it was simply because each of these men were using me as a toy at this point more than an actual woman.

Another endless burst of seed, another surge of heat, another risk taken. Even with all these men fucking me, and the amount they were coming, I should have known better than thinking me getting knocked up was a definite, but damn if it didn't feel so real at this point.

Ty withdrew from me, leaving me a lump of orgasm-riddled flesh.

"Three down, girl," Chris said, leaning into me. "You still got anything left in you?"

My response was some incoherent aching gurgle.

"That seems about right. We've done a number on her, but I still haven't had my proper turn."

"She's tight as hell, Chris," Ty called out. "Best fuck I've ever had. You're going to enjoy her."

Chris leaned down. "You didn't think you were going to escape with only my fingers fucking you, did you? How on earth do you think I was going to get you pregnant with only fingers? No, no, we have to do it right."

Oh god, their intent really was to knock me up. Having it happen by sheer chance was one thing, but the intent? It just made it all the more debaucherous of them to use me like this. Without even ever asking me, no less.

I might have tried to raise a protest if I had singlest iota of strength to do so.

Chris, though, was still going to get his. There was no 'too tired' in this situation. I still had a bill to pay, and my body was going to pay it.

He slid his cock along me, ready to find his way into the well-lubed slit that his friends had left behind.

And yet, even after everything that had happened, it still felt so damn good, so damn intense as he thrust himself inside of me. A tsunami rocking into me, even when I should have been absolutely drowned already.

Chris wrapped his arms fully around me, one hand tickling my breasts as he started to move with everything and begin to good and properly fuck me. Tweaking my breasts, wanting to get any life he could out of my nearly dead form. The feeling was still there, my body somehow still having a lick of energy left but still wanting to get going.

This time though, it wouldn't just be Chris fucking me. No. The other three were converging on my sorry form, all of their cocks beating hard and erect for me. Slick with their juices as well as my own.

With great willpower and effort, I guided my hands toward their cocks, knowing what they wanted, reading their sick, twisted, perverted minds.

All of them approaching me, my grip on them tightening, inching closer, jerking them with all my focus and effort on it. Ty and Greg in hand, it wasn't long until Ryan noticed I was shorthanded and put the rest of my body to work.

He grabbed me by the hair, pulled me up, and thrust his cock straight into my mouth, forcing me to taste the sweet mixture that was him and the rest of us going down. My heart was racing, realizing that I was pleasing four men at the same time, sucking on one, jerking two, all while I desperately tried to show any life at all for Chris as he fucked me.

I was absolutely the slut that they wanted me to be, exceeding my potential. There was a rush in being that sexual, that desired that I had never known before, and my sick twisted self liked it.

Soon though, it was all boiling over. Chris was so skillfully fucking me, a hand on my nipples and a hand on my clit. I was rising toward absolute bliss faster and faster, struggling to keep control of myself through it all, and yet he kept going. Kept fucking me.

As my hands were fucked, as my mouth was fucked.

The point of no return had been reached, and damn did it feel good to meet it.

Almost more explosive than anything I'd felt before, every nerve in my body flared in absolute delight. The ecstasy was my entire being at that moment.

I barely even felt Chris drop his load into the stew of cum that the rest of his friends left behind. I barely even felt that Ty and Greg had reached their climax once more, erupting into my hands, and all over my body. Ryan, reaching his limit, and exploding down my throat.

There was no way I could contain this, not then, maybe not ever. He too erupted out of my mouth and started to spray his seed all over me, all over my face.

There was laughter among all of them. It continued until Chris finally departed me and let me slump down into the mess on my bed.

It did seem odd at first why the movers went and made

my bed after doing everything else, but I guess it made a bit more sense as I thought about it. Still, I had to say I enjoyed it.

Nice sheets, a cover, readily made pillows. It was all very nice things for me to be able to pass out on.

"Damn she was good," Chris added. "You fuckers weren't lying. You're the best, Grace. We'll be happy to let you pay us like this any time you want."

There was a scramble for clothes. The job was done, they were spent, and there was nothing else for them to do. Getting dressed and getting ready to leave was only natural.

"The real shame is she has no real reason to call us again until she moves," Ty added.

"Well, if we're lucky, she might need a bigger apartment sooner than later," Greg said.

"Yeah, well, that'll still be nine months. Mighty long time to go without."

"We could call this a payment plan," Ryan shrugged. "Five payments of running the train on her."

"Let's not be so cutthroat," Chris patted his friend on the shoulder. "She earned every single cent she paid for this move."

"Damn right she did." Ryan stroked his chin. "Maybe we could encourage her to come and ask us to move a fridge slightly. Then we charge her full price."

They kept talking as they headed away, their voices fading. It was mostly trying to give me excuses to call them again, and not to let money be an obstacle.

I just smiled, my trembling hand going to my abdomen. The thought of it swelling from a night like this, a child born of such reckless love. It was such an enthralling thought.

My terrible misinterpretation of my new job's signing bonus might well have been the best mistake I ever made.

I would definitely be making similar mistakes again, that was for sure.

THE END

GET ACCESS TO OVER 20 MORE FREE EROTICA DOWNLOADS AT SHAMELESS BOOK DEALS

Shameless Book Deals is a website that shamelessly brings you the very best erotica at the best prices from the best authors to your inbox every day. Sign up to our newsletter to get access to the daily deals and the Shameless Free Story Archive!

DEAR DIARY BY CASSANDRA ZARA

Dear Diary, I know it's been a while since I wrote in you, but I didn't know how to tell you what happened. You see, I went to this party, and one thing led to another, and suddenly I was naked. There were four men there, and they liked my body. Soon, all four of them were using me, hard and unprotected. And you'll never believe what happened next!

*A*s you know, Diary, having my birthday at the end of May meant that I could have my birthday party on the last day of school. In years past, I'd have a small sleepover with girls from my class, and they'd all just ride the bus home with me that evening. However, now that I was graduating high school and turning eighteen on the same day, I needed to do something a bit bigger.

I hand-wrote all sixty invitations and handed them out to my entire senior class during the last couple weeks of school. I gave out nearly all of them on the first day, with a few more trickling out over the next couple weeks. There was only one that I hadn't been able to give out though.

Dan Townsend.

I didn't know if he didn't show up for the last couple weeks of classes or if I just hadn't seen him. I didn't give it much thought. But as I left for my high school graduation ceremony, I made sure to grab his invitation.

When I got there, I chatted up my friends, making sure that some of them were coming. There were a lot of parties going on that day, and I tried not to show my disappointment when people said that they probably couldn't come. Still, at least a few people said they planned to show up.

I saw Dan sitting at the end of a row, arms crossed and looking bored. I walked up to him. At least he was dressed in his graduation robes. I hadn't seen him outside of his leather jacket all year.

"Hey, Dan," I said as I walked up to him.

He looked up at me. "Oh, hey. Kim, right?"

I smiled and nodded. I didn't really care that he didn't know my name. We hadn't shared a single class since we started high school. Sure, he was cute, in a bad boy kind of way, but I didn't think we were very compatible. I was ninth in my class, while I wasn't even sure he was going to graduate until I saw his name on the ceremony program's list. "Here you go," I said, holding out the invitation.

"What's this?" he asked. He didn't take the invitation.

"It's an invitation to my graduation party, which is also my birthday party," I said.

"Will there be booze?" he asked immediately.

I kept the smile plastered on my face. "No, sorry!"

He looked at it warily, then slowly reached out and grabbed it. "I'm touched you thought of me," he said sarcastically.

"Well, you know, high school graduation is definitely

special. It's something to be shared with everyone," I said nervously.

"Shared with everyone, huh?" he asked, reading the invitation. "Mind if I bring a friend?"

"Oh, don't worry about that. I invited everyone in our class."

"I wasn't thinking of anyone from our class," he said.

I bit my lip. I didn't really want a party open to everyone. Still, what was one more person? "Sure! The more the merrier."

He laughed. "The more the merrier," he agreed. He took a quick glance up and down my body, quickly, as if he were trying to hide it. At the time, I noticed it, but I didn't think anything of it. I was oblivious to all signs of attraction from the boys at my school, which was probably why I was still a virgin.

"See you there!" I said as I hurried away to sit in my seat.

I SHIFT my body to get more comfortable. I reread what I wrote in my diary a moment ago. It's amazing how much I remember from that day.

I finally find a comfy position and continue writing.

THE GRADUATION CEREMONY went as planned, and we all left to get ready for the evening. I went home and immediately changed into my cutest white sundress with yellow flowers on it. I wore the bra that pushed my breasts up a little bit, and a white thong that wouldn't leave underwear lines under my dress. My mom let me use her makeup, so I applied a little blush, some lipstick, and some mascara. I was a grown-up now, officially eighteen years old and graduated from high school, and it was time for me to look like it.

People started showing up immediately, less than I had hoped for, but at least family came. I had made it clear that there was no alcohol here which was probably why my party wasn't full. Still, I got some presents from grandparents and distant cousins which would make college a little easier.

My friend Janet was the last teenager there. She was wearing a conservative skirt, but her top hugged her body tightly. Even with my push-up bra, her tits were bigger than mine. I had to admit I envied that her body was more womanly than mine was. "Should we go to another party?" she asked.

I bit my lip. I felt bad leaving my own party, but there was nothing else for me to do here. I nodded. "Let me go tell my mom."

I went inside and found my mom. "Mom, is it okay if I go to another party with Janet?"

Mom turned from the aunts she was talking to. I knew she liked Janet and thought she was a good influence on me. "Okay, but make sure to stay with Janet. Be careful. Don't drink, and if you feel unsafe, just leave the party."

"Okay," I said, intending to follow her instructions to the letter.

When I got back, Janet was being talked to by two boys. I only recognized one of them. He was wearing his trademark leather jacket.

"Hey, Dan," I said as I approached. "Glad you could make it."

Both boys turned toward me. Now I could see that the guy with Dan wasn't a high schooler. He was a man. And his eyes grew wide when he saw me. He looked me up and down, not even bothering to hide it a little bit. I know I said I was oblivious, but it was impossible not to notice this time.

The man rubbed his hand across his stubbly face. "Glad you invited us," he said in a rough voice, then did another once-over of my body.

I didn't know what to make of that. I hadn't invited this guy. I didn't have any idea what to say. Luckily, Dan jumped in. "Kim, I want you to meet Rick. He's my manager at work."

Somehow, having a name to the face put me at ease. I held out my hand to shake it. "Hi, Rick!" I said cheerfully.

Instead of shaking my hand, Rick grabbed it, then gave it a kiss. I gasped as I felt the roughness of his five o'clock shadow brush the soft skin of my fingers. When he finished kissing my hand, he practically growled at me. "Pleasure to meet you."

I stood there awkwardly. He didn't let go of my hand. I had to pull back for him to finally let it go.

"Well, sorry to tell you this, but we were about ready to go to another party," Janet said.

Rick's eyes darted back over to Janet. He gave her a once-over too, then shook his head dismissively. "Yeah, Dan told me you didn't have any booze here," he said.

I winced. What else had Dan told this guy about me?

"We'll see you guys later," I said softly.

"Now wait a minute," Rick said. "Maybe we're going to the same party. Where are you headed?"

I looked at Janet, and she looked at me. I didn't even know if she had a party picked out yet, but I definitely wasn't sure about telling this guy. "We don't know yet," I said.

Rick never even looked over at me. "Perfect. Tell you what. I know of another party nearby. More private. Hop in my car and we'll head over there." Rick's eyes watched Janet warily, like she was a piece of meat and he was a hungry predator.

"You're ready to go to the private party already?" Dan asked his friend.

"Yeah," he said, his eyes still on Janet. "You got to come here like you wanted, and I got something I want too."

I shrugged. "What do you think, Janet?"

"I don't think we should," she said.

"Come on," Dan said to me. "I've wanted to talk to you for a while, and this will be our chance."

I was frozen. Dan wanted to talk to me? He'd never showed any interest before... or maybe he had? And I just never noticed it? It was impossible to know.

"Okay..." I said softly.

"Kim, no!" Janet said.

I turned to Janet. "Just for a little while, and then we can go."

Janet crossed her arms over her body, pushing her tits up a little bit as she did. "Fine," she said with a pouty voice.

"That's the spirit," Rick said. He wrapped his arm around Janet and started to lead her away. I followed, and Dan was right there beside me.

I'M TAKING a quick pee break, Diary. I'll be right back.

Okay, where was I? Oh yeah, the car ride over.

"SIT in the back with your girl," Rick said. "I want Janet up here with me."

I blushed at him calling me "your girl". I expected Dan to object, but he didn't. He just looked down and blushed himself.

Rick led us to a beat-up old station wagon. I got in the back seat behind Janet and Dan got in on the other side. A moment later and we were off.

"I'm really glad you invited me to your party," Dan said.

"I'm really glad you came," I said. We sat there in nervous silence for a moment. "Are you going off to college next year?"

"No. I've got a good job here, and I like it here," he said.

"Oh," I said. "I'm going up to State University."

"That should be fun," he said. "I guess this is your last night in town then, right?"

"No, I'll be spending all summer here before going up," I said.

"Oh, that's good."

I knew I was overthinking things, but I overthought that. Was he happy to hear that I'd be here all summer?

"Stop it," Janet said from the front seat.

"What's wrong?" I asked. I could see Rick's hand stretched across toward her seat, but I couldn't see what was going on.

"Rick just snapped my bra strap," she said.

"So," Dan said, interrupting. "That's a pretty dress you have on."

I turned back to him, blushing. He liked my dress? "Thanks." I thought about what to add to that. Eventually I just blurted out, "I like your jacket."

He puffed up a bit, obviously proud of his jacket. "Why didn't you ever tell me that you liked my jacket?"

I froze. I mean I didn't really like his jacket. "Um, I guess I never had the chance."

"Well you have the chance tonight," he said. "I'm having a good time talking to you."

I smiled and was about to talk more when Janet squealed again. "Knock it off!"

"Come on, they're so nice," Rick said.

"I'm not that kind of girl," Janet said.

"Fine," Rick said. I wanted to know what was going on, but I was a bit distracted by Dan.

"Thanks," I said. I wasn't sure I was enjoying talking to him quite as much, but it was whatever. We'd be at another party soon.

Dan must have taken that to be an invitation because he leaned in and kissed me. I wasn't expecting it at all, and I didn't even open my lips. It was an awkward kiss, and he must have noticed that. However, he just kept going, and I didn't stop him. Eventually, I parted my lips a little bit, and he slipped his tongue in my mouth. He put his hand on the back of my neck and drew me in closer, and I let him. I had no idea he liked me at all, and I was enjoying the attention.

"Yeah, you like that, don't you?" I heard Rick say from the driver's seat.

I thought he was talking to me, so I whispered "yes" into Dan's mouth as we kissed.

He wasn't talking to me, though. "I told you, over the underwear," Janet said.

I broke from the kiss and looked at the front seat. Rick's hand was on Janet still, but lower now. I leaned forward and looked. Janet's face was contorted in a look of pleasure, and her skirt had ridden up. Rick's hand was up her skirt, rubbing her panties back and forth. Janet let out a little moan and gripped the side of her seat hard.

I gasped. I had never seen sex before, and I especially never expected to see my best friend having sex. I leaned back in my seat. "Shouldn't you be keeping your eyes on the road?" I asked.

Rick laughed. "My eyes are on the road... mostly." He looked back at us. "What do you think Dan? Do you want me to take us around the block again?"

Dan looked at me. He clearly wanted to keep kissing me. "I think you should go straight to the party."

"Okay, we're almost there," he said.

~

I'M BACK, Diary. I just had to go get a snack. There's a jar of pickles in the fridge, and it's been calling my name all day.

Where was I? Oh yeah. The apartment.

~

WE PULLED into the parking lot of a set of cheap apartments. I knew a lot of college students lived in these, but I was happy that I would be staying in the dorms next year.

Janet was out of the car first, fixing her skirt. She looked flustered.

"Are you okay?" I asked.

She shrugged. "Let's ditch these guys at the party as soon as we can," she said.

I nodded, though I wasn't sure why she let Rick play with her panties if she didn't want him to. I looked over at the two guys. Rick stuck his finger under Dan's nose and Dan recoiled. "Hey girls, hurry up," he yelled to us.

I put my arm around Janet while we walked. Rick tried to pull Janet to his side while we walked, but she clung to me. I was happy to provide her with the support she needed.

We went into the apartment building and went into one of the upstairs apartments.

It was disgusting. Beer bottles were everywhere, along with massive piles of crumbs. A filthy couch sat in front of a TV, with two guys sitting on it watching South Park. There were holes in the walls, like someone had punched them.

It was definitely a bachelor pad.

Worst of all, there didn't seem to be a party here at all. It was just four guys and us.

"I thought you were going to bring four back, Boss," one of the guys on the couch said.

"This is all we got," Rick said. He turned back to us. "Can I get you two ladies a beer?"

"Where's the party?" Janet asked immediately.

"It hasn't started yet, but it will," Rick said. "Beer?"

I shook my head and looked at Janet. She bit her lip, but then smiled at Rick. "Do you have a Mike's Hard Lemonade?"

"Fresh out," he said.

"Then I'll have a beer," she said.

"That's the spirit," Rick said. He turned to me. "And you, what's-your-face?"

"Kim," Dan said.

"Yeah, Kim. Do you want a beer?"

"No thank you," I said. I couldn't stand the taste of beer. In fact, I was surprised that Janet had said yes to it.

"Suit yourself." He went to the fridge and grabbed two beers, then opened them both. He sat on the couch and scooted the two guys over, leaving only enough room on the end for one person. "Come here, Janet."

Janet looked at me, then reluctantly separated from me to go sit next to Rick. I watched her accept the beer, then take a big gulp of it.

Dan grabbed my hand. "I was hoping we could talk some more," he said.

We hadn't talked much in the car, but I had a feeling that wasn't what he wanted anyway. Still, I followed him to the kitchen table. It was covered in mail and beer bottles. I sat down at the least dirty looking chair, and Dan sat next to me. He didn't waste a moment. He leaned in and started to kiss me again.

I ran my hand up his chest. Under that leather jacket, I could feel some hard muscles. I began to squirm a little bit in the chair. I hadn't really noticed how hot he was, and I was glad he thought I was hot too.

He started to breathe heavier as we kissed. His hands

gripped my sides through the dress. I couldn't help it. I wanted more. And so when his hands started to bunch my dress up, hiking my dress up past my underwear, I let him, even though I knew I shouldn't.

That's when Janet stormed up to me. "Come on, Kim. We're leaving."

I broke from the kiss. "What's wrong?" I pulled my dress back down, embarrassed that she had seen me like this.

"Rick won't keep his hands off of me," she said. "We can find another party."

I looked at Dan. His eyes were pleading with me to stay, and I wanted to listen. I turned back to Janet. "Can't we stay just a little bit longer?"

"Kim!" she said. "I'm leaving now, whether you do or not."

"Janet, I..." I didn't know what to do. Here was a guy who said he liked me, who obviously found me sexy. I wanted to explore this a little more.

"I'll drive her to the next party myself," Dan said.

"Are you bringing Rick?" Janet asked.

"No," Dan said. "It'll just be me and Kim."

She crossed her arms over her body, pushing up those tits of hers again. I knew she'd find someone who liked her at any party she went to, but I might not be so lucky. "Please," I said.

She rolled her eyes and looked like she was going to give me a sarcastic reply, but just then Rick walked up to her and grabbed her arm. "Yeah, baby. Just stay a little while longer."

"Ew, gross!" she screamed. She shrugged him off and stormed out the door of the apartment.

"Come back! I didn't mean anything!" Rick yelled, going after her.

I watched them both leave and bit my lip. My mom had told me to stay with Janet, and now she was leaving. I knew I should leave with her. I turned to tell Dan that I had to go, but before I could talk, he pressed his lips against mine and started kissing me again.

My worries melted away. As his hands explored my body, I knew I wanted to stay here with him. And his hands did explore. In a few more moments, he had hiked my dress back up around my waist, exposing my thong panties completely.

The world faded away around me, which is why it was just a shock when Rick kicked Dan's chair. "Get your jacket back on, we're going to another party," he said.

I looked up at Rick, then back at Dan. I hadn't even noticed that he had taken his jacket off, leaving just a white shirt on underneath. "What happened?" Dan asked.

"That bitch took off, what does it look like?" Rick said, obviously angry.

I didn't like that he called my best friend a bitch. Dan looked pale himself. "Um, I think I'll just stay here," he said softly.

"What?" Rick asked. He sounded a little menacing.

"I'll just stay here with Kim. You can go to another party by yourself," Dan said.

"I told you, I can't go to high school parties by myself. I'll look like a weirdo," Rick said. "With you there, I'm the cool older friend."

Dan swallowed. "I'd really like to stay here."

"Look, I get it. You have a crush on this slut, and I went to her party first. For you. And we can come back after we get another slut for me."

Dan looked stunned. "I... I... I..."

Rick didn't let him finish. He turned to me. "Man, I don't blame you. This one definitely has a sweet and innocent thing going for her." He stood next to me and ran his fingers through my hair. "Maybe we don't have to go anywhere after all."

Dan sighed and looked relieved. "Look, I'll make it up to

you. We'll go to a party tomorrow."

Rick kept rubbing his hand through my hair. "Oh, definitely. Probably later tonight. But first, you don't mind sharing, do you?"

My eyes went wide. I stared at Dan. How come I didn't get a say in this? Would Dan share me like this?

"No, I don't think I can share her, Rick," he said.

For a moment, Rick closed his fingers on my hair, like he was going to pull it. Then he relaxed and let go. "Dan, I can't believe what I'm hearing. Who got you an easy, high-paying job?"

Dan sighed. "You did, Rick."

"And who's the coolest manager there is?"

"You are, Rick."

"And who asked for just the smallest favor so that he could pick up some high school chicks tonight?" Rick asked. He left my side and started toward Dan.

"You did, Rick."

He reached out and grabbed Dan by the face with one hand, squeezing his cheeks together. "And who's going to share the high school chick he got?"

Dan hesitated. "I am, Rick."

I wanted to run, but then Rick turned his eyes to me. I could see how badly he wanted me, and it turned me on.

I looked at Dan, and he shrugged. "The more the merrier, right?" he said, echoing the words I had used earlier during the graduation ceremony.

I wasn't so sure I agreed right now.

"Keep kissing her," Rick said, then shoved Dan's face toward mine. For a moment, our faces were pressed together without kissing, but we opened our mouths and began kissing. "Beautiful," Rick said.

I liked being called beautiful. I liked Dan's kisses. My mind was swimming, but I couldn't stop myself. So when I felt Rick's fingers moving my dress down, I didn't stop him. I didn't stop him when he undid my bra either.

"These are cute," he said, pinching my nipples hard. He was being a little too rough, so I slapped his hand away. "Oh, she's a fighter too." He slipped his hand under my nose, making me smell it. It smelled like mine did after I masturbated. "Let's see if you like this as much as your friend did."

I recoiled. I didn't want to smell that, especially knowing that it was Janet's essence. Still, as Dan pulled me close, I calmed down.

"Have her suck your dick," Rick said.

Without hesitation, Dan pulled his pants down. My eyes went wide. I had never seen a penis that hard and big in my entire life.

Dan brought me in for one last kiss. "I am so into you right now," he said.

I melted into him at the sound of those words. I didn't even resist when Rick pushed my face down, and I accepted it into my mouth. Rick pulled the chair out from under me, and I would have fallen to the ground if he hadn't caught me by the arm. He gently lowered me, and I knelt down, continuing sucking on Dan's dick.

As I sucked, I looked up at Dan. He was obviously loving it. He pulled his shirt off and I could see those muscles that I had felt earlier.

I was so engrossed with Dan that I barely felt Rick hike my dress up so that it was bunched around my belly, then pull my panties down. I didn't notice until I felt his stubbly face on my ass cheeks, moments before I felt his tongue.

"Oh my God," I moaned as I felt his tongue start at my clit, go all the way down my pussy, then down further and lick my asshole. He did that again and again, those long tongue strokes feeling amazing as he tasted me from end to end.

"She tastes just like a peach," he said to Dan.

Dan just grunted and kept looking at me as I sucked on his dick. I felt Rick move away, then I felt his hands spread my ass apart further. I thought he was going to lick me some more, but then I felt a new pressure against my entrance. I realized it was his cock, and that he was about to fuck me.

I moved my hands back to stop him, then looked back. "You can't!" I cried out.

"Baby, you liked it when it was my tongue," Rick said. He kept trying to push in.

"That was different. I'm..." I trailed off, then spoke up. "I'm a virgin."

"Yeah right," he said, then pressed into me the rest of the way. I felt my opening spread further as he pushed further in, tearing my virginity away callously for his own pleasure. I cried out, then collapsed into Dan's lap.

⌒

So THAT's how I lost my virginity, Dear Diary. I didn't expect it to be on the sticky floor of some dirty apartment, but that's how it happened.

I could end the story here, but it feels incomplete. I'm not sure how much more I should write, but somehow I feel like I should tell you the whole story. I'm going to have to look back on this, to remember it, in the future, so I might as well be as complete as possible.

⌒

"OH MAN," Rick said. "She's about as tight as a virgin though."

"Can't wait to have a turn," Dan said.

I looked up at him, feeling a little betrayed right about

now. Rick grabbed my hair and shoved my face back into Dan's lap. "Keep sucking him," he commanded.

I did as he ordered, even though I was holding back tears from being fucked so roughly. Dan was even harder now, fucking my mouth, and he was hitting that little dangly thing in the back of my throat.

Time seemed to melt away, but it did seem like only a little time had passed before I heard a frantic set of grunts behind me. I felt a hot explosion inside me, filling me up completely. With every thrust, more of the hotness filled me, permeating into every crevice of my body.

Then he pulled out. I was confused.

"You came already?" Dan asked, laughing a little.

"Shut the fuck up," Rick said. "This little whore was too tight. I couldn't help myself."

He came inside of me? I reached back, feeling a sticky mess as I ran my fingers over my opening. It was dripping onto the floor already, and more of it was coming out.

"It doesn't matter," he said. "You are on birth control, right?"

I hadn't been thinking straight. Of course I wasn't on birth control. I had never even been kissed by a guy, let alone fucked. My face paled at the thought of becoming pregnant with this guy's child. I looked back and shook my head.

Rick ran his fingers through his hair. I could see the sweat that had beaded on his forehead while he had fucked me. "This is bad. I can't knock another girl up."

Another girl? How many times had he done this?

"Can she shower it out?" Dan asked.

"Nah, I shot it way too deep inside of her." He ran his hand through his hair again, then slowly looked toward the other room. I had forgotten about the two guys there, but they hadn't forgotten about us. They were openly staring at us, giggling and whispering and pointing.

"I've got an idea," Rick said. He reached down and grabbed me by the arm. With my virginity being torn from me, I was having trouble walking, but Rick didn't seem to care. "Looks like I did get a girl for you two after all."

He threw me down on the couch between the two guys. I was basically naked still, my dress pressed into a thin line of fabric hanging on top of my hips.

"Aw, thanks Boss," one of the guys said. He already had his pants off, so he was just wearing a shirt. He knelt down in front of the couch and spread my legs open.

I was feeling too weak, too out of it, to fight it. Didn't I have any say in this? The way this guy was pawing at me, the answer was clearly no.

With my legs spread open, the guy had an easy time slipping his cock into my pussy, especially with all of Rick's semen lubing me up. And almost immediately, sex with this man felt a lot less painful. Within moments, I was writhing in front of him, undulating my body so that his cock hit all the right spots.

"Fuck, you were right Rick, she's tight," the man said.

I took that as a compliment. I wrapped my hands around the back of the guy's neck to give me leverage so that I could undulate on his cock, feeling him hit every internal inch of me.

I noticed the guy next to us had gotten naked, so I reached over and grabbed his cock. I didn't really know how to jerk a guy off, so I just held onto it. I felt him get harder and harder as he watched me fuck the other guy.

"Have her come over and sit on my cock for a little bit, will ya?" the other guy said.

"Nah, man. She feels too good," the guy fucking me said.

I smiled at that.

"Come on, we all know you're an ass guy anyway."

The guy fucking me laughed, then seemed to strain

himself to fuck me harder. Then he pulled out of me. "You're right," he said with another laugh.

The guy to my side grabbed onto the hand that was holding onto his dick, then pulled me over to him. I turned over and straddled him, and that cock slammed right into my pussy. I recoiled a little from the shock of it, then eased down onto it when I saw the look on his face.

"Fuck, she's incredible," the guy underneath me said.

I felt the guy who had been exploring me spread my ass cheeks open. "Looks like she's already ready for me," he said.

I thought about how Rick had flicked his tongue against my asshole a few times, but I was nowhere near ready. As I felt him line up his dick with my ass, I feebly reached back to try and stop him.

"Hey, grab her arms, will ya?" the guy behind me said.

The guy in front of me pulled me down to him, kissing me on the lips as he pinned my hands behind my back. I moaned into his mouth as the guy behind me pressed his dick into my ass, spreading me wider than I ever expected to be spread.

YES, it's true, Diary. I let two complete strangers, who I never even learned their names, have sex with me that day. I let them split me, one of them in my ass and one in my pussy. My brain was crying 'no' but my body was absolutely singing 'yes'.

FOR A MOMENT, I tried to fight getting split by the guy behind me. However, the guy in front of me was still pinning my arms behind my back. My mouth gaped open as I collapsed even further down onto him.

I had never felt fuller than I did with two men using my ass and my pussy.

"She's even tighter with you in her ass," the guy underneath me said.

The guy behind me laughed. "You're so gay," he said.

"Maybe, but you're the one fucking her ass."

"Mmm, it's such a nice ass too." The man behind me pressed down on my back and began to rail into me even harder. I moaned as I struggled against him. "You ready for me to come?"

I hardly wanted him to come in my ass, but I knew the alternative could be worse. "Yes," I said.

"Oh yeah. Tell me you want it," he said.

"I want it," I said.

"Beg for it."

"Please. Please come in my ass. Please!" I screamed.

"Oh yeah, that's pretty hot," the guy below me said.

"Oh yeah," the guy behind me agreed. I could feel him push down even harder on my back as he railed into me. With the guy below me also thrusting into me, I could feel a wave of intense pleasure building within me. I lost all control. I squeezed my eyes shut and surrendered to their actions.

"Yeah, you gonna come for me, baby?"

I didn't know which one of them said it, but it didn't matter. I couldn't respond. My body opened to their thrusts and I felt my legs begin to shake.

"Yeah, she's coming," one of them said.

"I'm about to join her," the other said.

I couldn't stop myself from moaning as he said that. My eyes were still squeezed shut, and I heard a whine come from my mouth as I felt the man behind me swell and release into me. Deep within my bowels, I felt a hot splash fill me. My orgasm never stopped during this, and I felt my ass contract and relax on him, milking him for everything he had.

When he pulled out of me, I felt a rush of fluid come out of me. I moaned again.

The guy below me let go of my arms. He pulled out of me and I felt his cock quest around my asshole. For a moment, I thought he was going to put it in my ass also. However, he just rubbed his cock all around the liquid streaming from me, coating his cock in it.

"That'll lube her up nicely," he said.

"Haha, you are so gay," the other guy said as he sat down beside us. He had the remote in his hand. "Can I unpause this yet?"

"Give me a minute, I'm almost done," he said. He slipped his cock back inside me, and I could feel the new warmth fill my pussy as he thrusted. Without the guy in my ass, it felt way less intense. However, he began to pound into me with a new energy.

I put my hands on his chest as he pressed deeply within me. When his hands went to my tits, I arched my back. That seemed to do it for him, and when he pinched my nipples, I could feel his cock grow even more.

"Oh yeah," he said, biting his lip. He cupped my boobs and pushed them up and down. I put my hands on his pecs and spurred him on, feeling another eruption inside of me as he lost control and came inside of me. His seed mingled with the other two men's and re-coated my insides.

I bounced on him for a few more seconds while he recovered. Finally, he opened his eyes, then looked past me.

"You can unpause it," he said as he lifted me off of him. I gasped as their seed flowed out of my body. I didn't have a lot of time to let it flow before he tossed me off of him and onto the couch. My legs remained open, and I looked down to see the mess that the three men before had left in me.

I moved my hand to my clit, rubbing myself slowly as I recovered. I had been used and abused already, but as I looked up at the last man in the room, I knew I wasn't done yet.

~

THAT'S RIGHT, Diary. I had already been inseminated by three strangers, but there was still one more man there. The man who had lured me there. The man who, if I had to choose, I'd choose to be impregnated by.

I'll be back in just a moment, Diary. I have to pee again.

~

DAN WAS SITTING on the arm of the couch, looking down on me. He was looking at me with what I assumed was a mixture of disgust and arousal.

I kept rubbing my clit as I looked up at him, the warm, sticky fluid creating a fantastic sensation. "Dan," I said.

I assumed he'd jump at the chance to pound into me, but he hesitated. He still had his clothes off, and I noticed that he had... deflated a little bit.

I couldn't imagine how I would still feel pretty if he rejected me now. I tried to get to my feet, but my abdominal muscles didn't seem to want to work. It was taking all I had just to hold it together, but I had to have him.

I had to feel Dan within me.

I rolled over and laid on my stomach, then beckoned him toward me. My feet laid across one of the men who had just used me, but he was just fixated on the TV. Dan knelt on the couch in front of me, and I propped myself up on my elbows.

I took him in my mouth. Just a few minutes ago, I sucked him like an amateur, but now I sucked him off with reckless abandon.

He grew in my mouth as I sucked. In a few moments, he had his hands on the back of my head, running his fingers through my hair again. He got hard again immediately. For a moment, I thought he might come inside my mouth. Although that meant he wouldn't come inside my pussy, I found it incredibly hot.

"Not yet," Rick said, clapping Dan hard on the shoulder. I felt him deflate a little bit again. "I need you to do it in here."

He reached down to my ass, then slipped his fingers into my pussy. I felt him roughly push some of the semen back into my pussy as he fingered me.

"Yeah," Dan said. "Of course."

"Of course what?" Rick prompted.

"Of course... Boss," Dan said.

"Good," Rick said. He took a seat on the other side of the guys, then looked back at us. "Go on," he insisted.

Dan pulled out of my mouth and stood up, looking at me. He looked like he was going to try and mount me while I was prone, but then he looked at the other men he'd have to crawl over. He was already deflating a little more.

I decided to make it a little easier for him. At great effort to myself, I rolled back over on my back, facing the TV. I bent my knees up, then looked back up at him and bit my lip.

Looking down on me, I could tell he liked what he saw. I bit my lip and beckoned him with my finger. He slid into me, easily breaching into my already tenderized body. I moaned with surprise pleasure as he plowed into me.

He immediately got hard, and he was definitely bigger than any of the other men. He hit spots that none of the other men had been able to, and as his cock plowed into me, I felt my hand immediately go to my clit.

I arched my back, somehow finding the energy to writhe. His hands went to my sides, rubbing up and down. "God, you're beautiful," he said.

I looked up at him. "Really?" I asked him.

"Really," he said. "I've wanted you for years now."

I felt warm inside, and it had nothing to do with the hot semen permeating my body. "Why didn't you say anything?" I asked.

"I was too nervous to talk to you," he said. He looked down at my pussy, and at the hot liquid that was being pulled out of me with every thrust that he made. "I'm sorry that it took this to get us together."

I thought about that for a moment, through the haze of the pleasure and pain running through my body. I looked over at Rick, who had wanted me for nothing more than his own pleasure.

Some might be mad at him for stripping away their virginity, but I knew that, without him, Dan would never have worked up the nerve to talk to me.

I turned back to Dan and rubbed my clit even harder. "Come in me, Dan. Come inside my pussy," I demanded.

Dan looked at me like I was the most beautiful woman he had ever seen. Sweat beaded on his brow as he pounded into me. I could feel my pleasure rising as he made me feel pretty.

I felt my pussy clamp down on him as his seed flowed into me. And this time, my body contracted, my muscles drawing his semen further into my body. I wanted it all inside of me. I wanted it to stay in me. I wanted it to claim my body.

My orgasm kept going as he pumped every last bit of his seed into me. He collapsed into me, and I wrapped my arms around his back, keeping him in me as closely as possible.

I felt like we could have stayed this way forever. That was until Rick came back and spanked Dan on the ass. "Come on, get out of that slut. We got a lot more strange to tame tonight."

Dan put a little distance between us. He was looking me in the eye. "She's not a slut," he said without looking up at him.

Rick laughed, a mean laugh. "Oh okay, yeah, fall in love with the first whore you nut in. That's a good idea."

Dan sighed and pulled out of me. I gasped but pulled my legs up in the air to try to hold as much of his seed as I could. He looked down at my body, and for a moment, I thought he was thinking that I was a whore.

"Both of you, get your clothes on," Rick said. Dan got up and started to pull his clothes on. I willed my body to move, but I was still too tender. "You too, unless you want to stay the night here."

I looked over at the dingy couch, and at the two men who would probably love to have another go at my tight little body. I shook my head and stood up. I staggered over to the kitchen table and grabbed my panties and bra, putting them on as quickly as possible while Rick watched me. I pulled my dress to where I thought it was when I got here, but no matter how I adjusted it, it just didn't feel right. I wondered if they had stretched the fabric so that it no longer fit, or if they might have stretched my body instead.

When I was dressed, Rick grabbed his keys. "Good. Now which party did your friend Janet run off to?"

I shook my head. "I don't know."

"Well, text her and find out. We'll drop you off at your house on our way over there."

I pouted. "Can't I come with you?"

Dan looked at my face, then opened his mouth as if to speak. Then he closed it and looked at Rick, as if to say, "you tell her."

Rick laughed. "You can come if you want, but you might

want to go to the bathroom and take a look at yourself in the mirror first."

I wanted to go to the bathroom bad, but I wanted to do it at home, where I could really cleanse my body. Still, I wanted to see what they saw. I limped to the bathroom and looked at my face in the mirror. I immediately regretted using my mother's makeup. My lipstick was smeared and my mascara was running. I looked like a clown.

The bathroom was too filthy for me to clean myself in, but I did use some water to clear away some of the makeup. When I came back out, Rick laughed his mean laugh again. "Still want to party with us?"

I shook my head.

"Good. Did you ask your friend Janet where she was?"

I shook my head, but before he could ask me again, I lied. "She said she doesn't want to see you."

Rick looked furious for a second, then calmed himself. "Yeah, I had a feeling that might be the case. Okay, Dan. You find the next party for us."

Dan looked at me, then back at Rick, and just nodded. I sighed inwardly. Dan had obviously just been saying those things, though why he had bothered, I would never know. He was already inside of me. I was already going to let him come inside of me. He had lied to me for no reason.

It was the final betrayal of the evening, but it was the one that hurt the most.

In a daze, I found myself in the back of the car. Rick drove while Dan sat in the front seat, texting people to find out where the next party was. Where the next slut for them was.

THEY DROPPED ME OFF, *Diary, and I snuck into my house without anyone seeing me. I washed myself as best I could. I went to bed early that night, thinking that would be the end of it.*

It turned out, Rick drank too much at the next party and made a huge scene. I never got the whole story, but I got the feeling that Dan confronted him, or otherwise cock-blocked him from using another girl like he had used me.

Rick's a wanted man now. He's on the run, but they're pretty sure he isn't around here. I don't think it was for fighting at the party though. I think one of the other girls he got with went to the cops.

I got a knock on my door the next day, the first day of summer break. A clean-cut man wearing a button-up shirt had flowers for me. I hardly recognized him without the trademark leather jacket, but he said he was turning over a new leaf, and that he refused to turn into an asshole like Rick.

I believed him, Diary. Lord knows why, but I believed him.

He was promoted to the manager position that Rick had vacated when he fled town. He took me on real dates, and we made love nightly, though I insisted he use a condom each time.

That didn't last. Just as I was about to leave for college, I took a pregnancy test.

I THINK ABOUT WRITING MORE. About the serious talk I had with Dan. About the decision whether to keep it. About the fights with my parents. About my decision not to leave for college after all. In the end, I rub the belly that I rest my diary against. It's round, which doesn't make for the best writing surface, but it's as big as a desk, and it's more comfy to lay here on my bed while writing. I know that the future reader of this story doesn't need to hear all those other messy details.

. . .

My daughter's father is Dan, despite the other men there that night. He said that he'd treat her as his daughter no matter what. And I believed him.

I still believe him.

I love him.

He'll be here any minute to pick me up for my maternity appointment, so I better go. The only other thing I can tell you, Dear Diary, is that I'm sorry that it took nine months for me to write that all down. I hope to update you in a few days when our new life enters this world.

I put the diary down. I know I need to get my shoes on, but I feel like I left a detail out. That's impossible, of course. This diary entry practically qualifies as a piece of erotica at this point. Still, I open it to the beginning, and realize my mistake immediately. I cross out the sentence on the first line and write it again, right above where it had been written before. I rub my belly again, and read the line of the diary entry I'm sure I'll be reading again someday.

Something wonderful has happened.

THE END

GET ACCESS TO OVER 20 MORE FREE EROTICA DOWNLOADS AT SHAMELESS BOOK DEALS

Shameless Book Deals is a website that shamelessly brings you the very best erotica at the best prices from the best authors to your inbox every day. Sign up to our newsletter to get access to the daily deals and the Shameless Free Story Archive!

MORE FROM SHAMELESS BOOK PRESS

We have so many bundles for your enjoyment! Ranging from pseudo-incest and dubious consent to anal and lactation, we've got it!

With some of the best authors the genre has ever seen, most of the stories are exclusive to us, so you won't find them anywhere else!

CHECK out the Shameless Book Bundles available on Amazon!